Buffalo Man

An unsung hero, or a forgotten Legend.
Spawn from heights of heaven,
or recruited from the depths of hell.

Buffalo Man

An unsung hero, or a forgotten Legend.
Spawn from heights of heaven,
or recruited from the depths of hell.

a novel by

Michael Kellum

Pittsburgh, PA

ISBN 1-56315-285-1

Paperback Fiction
© Copyright 2002 Michael Kellum
All Rights Reserved
First Printing — 2002
Library of Congress #2001095142

Request for information should be addressed to:

SterlingHouse Publisher, Inc.
7436 Washington Avenue
Suite 200
Pittsburgh, PA 15218
www.sterlinghousepublisher.com

Book Designer: Beth Buckholtz
Cover Design: Jeffrey S. Butler — SterlingHouse Publisher, Inc.

This publication includes images from Corel Draw 8 which are
protected by the copyright laws of the U.S., Canada and elsewhere.

Printed in the United States of America

TABLE OF CONTENTS

CHAPTER 1

PURGATORY

12 July 0500, 1878 in the swamps of Buford, South Carolina.
The heat and humidity was unbearable. I'm sure both were at least 95 or better. I led my horse through the swamp of Buford S.C. Do you know what it's like to pull a horse through the swamp? Somewhere and sometime ago I quit worrying about the smaller friends of the swamp, such as the ticks, leeches, and mosquitoes. I figured they was as miserable as I was in these conditions. My horse seemed to be mainly annoyed by the flies, as his tail twitches and makes whip like sounds. His feeble attempts to fan himself draw even more company. I believe he is more miserable than I. His large frame provides varmints of all types with a temporary home. I dare not to jump on his back to ride him, because his strength is weakened with every step of the way, just like mine. Before I started this venture I had thought that the clothing on my back would offer some protection from the harsh elements of the swamp. I also figured that my special training in the Army would prepare me for this type of situation, mentally and physically, but it didn't. My wool pants have a gaping hole that allows different critters to nest in my crotch. The mosquitoes and the flies bore their way through my dark shirt and my skin absorbed the heat. My boots have become waterlogged, as the water and mud have found their way through the holes that had been developed over time. My straw-made plantation hat offers me little protection from the sun, and my suspenders cut into my shoulder blades, making it hard to keep my pants up. The

only protection my horse has from the elements is his saddle. The saddle, however, is weighed down with my equipment, including my pistol belt with a loaded Smith and Western 45s, a Sharps Sniper Rifle with attached scope, one sawed-off double-barreled shotgun, two cans of assorted ammo, two canteens of fresh water, one medical aid bag, and a quarter pouch filled with beef jerky.

It is said that life is a bitch and then you die. I felt that my environment was eating away at my spirit, slowly but surely. The depth of the water was initially ankle deep, but, after three hours of traveling with no end in sight, the water level was waist high and the mud began to get deeper. Every step was a challenge. The sun, the humidity, the bugs, the high water table, and now this damn mud was zapping my energy. Now I'm exerting my reserve to get through this damn mud. "Shit, now what? I've got a cramp in my leg," I cried. As luck would have it, my feet are sticking in the mud. My mind started to drift. I thought about quicksand. I thought, *what a miserable way to die. Death in this god forsaken shitty ass swamp.* Navigation through this hell hole is also difficult. I lost my pace count because of the underbrush in the swamp kept getting tangled in my feet. The large moss trees and the drifting cloud movement made it difficult to use the sun as a navigational tool. I sometimes felt that I was walking in a complete circle. I was tired but somehow I increased the pace. My intent was to make it to dry land before dark. Based on the sun's position and the heat it must had been mid-afternoon: at least one or two o'clock. Unfortunately the cooler temperatures would bring on the real dangers of the swamp. The cotton mouths and alligators normally hunt their prey around the latter part of the evening. With all these images running through my mind simultaneously, I tried to optimize and evaluate my current situation. I knew that if I slowed the pace down, my fate would be sealed within the confines of this swamp. I put myself in this situation for a purpose, and knew that there would be no turning back, because if I did, all would be lost.

An hour later the second wave of pain began. My feet were completely waterlogged and were as red and bloated as raw hamburger. I could feel the stinging sensation of small cuts between my toes. The blisters at the bottom of my feet had softened, and I'm sure that they were bleeding. My hands were rubbed raw from pulling my horse's leather bridle through the swamps. The wound that I suffered during the Indian wars ached. I constantly stopped to rub the cramps out of my hamstrings. Every time the cramps started, I knew that I was on the edge of heat exhaustion. Thus, I had to drink from my limited supply of fresh water. I'd average one to two caps every 1000 meters.

Sometimes I had to stop to reorient my direction of travel. I would focus on a distinct tree, and walk towards it, and then find something else unique to walk toward. This method was the only means that I had to navigate with.

I originally estimated the swamp to be at least 17 to 20 miles long from North to South. To the West was land, but at this moment dry land wouldn't offer me the concealment that I needed. To the east was the ocean. I couldn't be certain about the distance I had covered and my exact location. There was no sense in using the map that I had purchased from an old trading post, because it was outdated. I estimated that I had traveled at least five miles. However, fighting with the underbrush threw off my pace count. In any case, forward and straight as possible was the only direction that I was sure about because North was the only option.

Being alone out in the middle of nowhere made me a little crazy. I would have conversations with my horse and believed that he would talk back to me. "What else could possibly happen out here," I asked him. "I'm hot and hungry for some real food. I'm soaked from head to toe, my legs are cramping, this mud feels like quicksand, my blisters are bleeding, my wounds is aching, I'm running out of freshwater, and to top it off, I'm lost. So tell me, horse what the hell is next?" The horse was annoyed by the flies, and swung his whip-like tail at them. "Oh, I forgot about those damn flies." Moments later, the sun began to fade away. The sunshine was being replaced with large cumulous black clouds. I let out a sigh of relief because I figured that the cooler temperatures would provide me with some respite from the heat and humidity.The temperature did as I expected. The temperatures declined and I began to smell the rain. Again my optimistic side took over. "Look horse, smell that sweet rain water. Just think. You won't have to deal with those damn flies much longer." I said. The rain started as a mist, followed by a sweet and gentle Southerly breeze. An hour later, I glanced to the East and saw a distant darkening sky. "Oh shit." My jaw dropped in disbelief. An evil-looking storm front was moving in my direction from the East. I looked at the cloud movement to figure how fast this front was moving. It was easy to tell because there was a stark distinction between the gray and black clouds.There was nowhere to run for shelter. It was a simple matter of toughing it out. The wind and rain picked up. The thunder got closer and closer. There was occasional flares of lightning. I tried to pick up the pace but my feet kept getting tangled in the underbrush. There was no gradual buildup, as all three hit at the same time. Thick sheets of rain blocked my vision. The thunder sounded like cannon fire and the lighting dashed from the heavens to the earth. The water table begun to rise. My horse became rattled. I had to tug his bridle numerous times in order to gain control. I continued to move in a Northerly direction even though the level increased. At this point, the water level was chest deep, and my movement slowed to a snail's pace. The turbulence of the water slammed against my horse and it changed our direction. The swamp grass and the moss tree leaves blew in my face, and disrupted my vision. Twenty minutes had passed, and the storm front moved inland to the west.

I lost track of the time. It seemed like I'd been in this swamp forever. The swamp was beginning to play on my nerves. I felt that I was trapped in a tightly-enclosed room, but the swamp was large. Every bush, branch and tree look the same. I was not sure if I was traveling north. The storm screwed up my sense of direction. In any case, I couldn't see dry land in any direction. I depended on my directional instincts, and continued to move in whatever direction I felt was right. The temperature lowered and the thunder could be heard in the distant west. The overcast skies brought on a constant but hazy drizzle. I was wet, exhausted and lost, but the heat temperature wasn't extremely hot. My stomach had begun to cramp. The swamp was beginning to affect my body mentally and physically. The key to staying alive was to keep moving.

I began to reminisce about stories and fables that my grandparents used to tell me on their plight to freedom during the dark days of slavery. Slaves used to use swamps as an avenue of escape from their masters. I then began to compare my situation with theirs. If they were captured, they were beaten and lynched. Now I'm using a swamp to escape lynch mobs, bounty hunters, and supposedly the law. It was clear to me now why this purgatory was such an important escape route. The swamp offered cover and concealment. Tracking is next to impossible through this marsh, and dogs would never be able to pick up the scent. No sane man would follow anyone through this hellhole. However, I'm sure the survivability rate was low. *Yet the ill-equipped slaves survived, and so will I. I will survive,* I thought. With this thought in mind, I became focused once again. The drizzle turned into a London like haze. I figured it must be getting toward the latter part of the evening. The bullfrogs and crickets began to cry. The only other audible sound was my horse and I trudging through the swamp water. My mouth was dry, and my stomach once again ached with either diarrhea or hunger.

I stopped to eat. I drank two caps of fresh water from my canteens. I reached into my saddlebag to get out my pouch that had the beef-jerky. As luck would have it, the pouch was empty. I knew that it must have fallen out of my pouch during the storm, or maybe I'd already eaten it. I was on an emotional roller coaster. My spirits fell when I felt that empty pouch. Prior to moving out, I had ensured that everything was tied down, just in case of bad weather. After two or more hours had passed during my quest for freedom, trees became plentiful to the west. The once bright skies began to fade. The nightfall was just around the corner. There was something barely visible over the horizon. I squinted, hoping to see something favorable. I asked myself, "is it land or just an oasis? Could my mind be playing tricks on me again?" I cried out a deep sigh of relief once I confirmed that it was dry land. Finally, there was light at the end of the tunnel. An hour later, I reached the banks. I quickly moved inland. I pitched camp, started a fire for warmth, and prepared myself for a well-deserved rest. I laid down with my back against a moss tree while studying the outdated map, wondering where the hell I was. At this point it didn't matter. I threw the map to the ground and dwelled on the past, and how I'd gotten there.

CHAPTER 2

THE MARSHALL'S POINT OF VIEW

12 July

My name is Marshall Car. I'm the Regional Marshall in this area and other boarding territories. My office is located in the town of Greenville, which is 6 miles to the south of Buford.

Two of my deputies and I were playing out the last hand of poker for the night. I gulped down my chaser glass of whiskey and looked at my unfortunate hand of cards. I had a pair of threes, which meant that I was about to lose another game. Unlucky as I was, I'd decided to play this hand anyway.

Suddenly, I could hear footsteps outside the jail running up the wooden steps towards the door. There was an earsplitting beating on the door. Bam, bam, bam! "Marshall Car, wake up." Bam, bam, bam! "Marshall Car, wake up," the voice on the outside screamed. I quickly jumped out of my chair and gingerly ran barefooted towards the door. My two deputies beat me there first. They opened the door to find a black male who was about 16 years of age. When he stepped into the light, I recognized him. As the Marshall in this area, I know just about everyone who lives in this vicinity. "Aren't you old man Higgins' boy?" I asked. "Your daddy sharecrops corn and cotton for Mr. Miller." The young lad was profusely sweating and trying to catch his breath.

He began to state over and over between breath, "There gunfire and death out at Old Man McDowell place. Marshall, you've got to come now. There been gunfire out at Old Man McDowell place. And the fire,"

I interrupted the young lad, "what fire?"

I sat the boy down and handed him a cup of whiskey. He maniacally grabbed the bottle out of my hand and began to gulp down the whiskey.

One of my deputies grabbed back the bottle, "Marshall that's good whiskey he's wasting," the deputy said. I started the inquisition, "Ok son, take a deep breath and tell me what you saw."

The teenager was still trembling, but began to tell what he saw with a little more clarity. "This evening I woke up to use the outhouse. When I walked outside, I could see a distant brightness flashing out of the woods. I could smell smoke. I thought the cotton-field was on fire. I ran in the direction of the fire. It was so dark, I tripped over something soft. I looked down at what I tripped over, and it was a dead cow. I was on the edge of the fence-line and could see the rear of the McDowell's place. Everything was on fire. I could hear the crying of horses. They were being burned inside of the barn. I then saw some men running out of the house, firing their guns at someone or something. Someone from inside the house gunned them down. I thought that I'd be next. I took off running. Marshall, I was so scared for my life that I ran the whole way. It was cold blooded murder."

The deputy handed back the bottle of whiskey back to the teen. My deputies and I looked at each other in total silence for a minute. I had a hard time believing this story. Black Jack McDowell is one of the wealthiest landowners in this territory. He has at least 50 hired gunmen to oversee his operation. There was no telling how many people he had on his pay-role, because he owned a third of the town of Buford businesses. The real truth of the matter was, McDowell's problem really didn't concern me because McDowell was a criminal himself. He achieved his wealth by leeching off the unfortunate. His empire grew as his reign of terror spread throughout the valley. All of his gunmen and relatives were thugs, hooligans, and the scum of the earth. They don't respect the law, but they were the law in Buford, and they rule by terror. I hesitated, wondering why I should get involved. However, I was the US Marshall in this God-forsaken district, so I had to do something.

I instructed one deputy to saddle up the horses, and the other deputy to escort the town doctor out to the McDowells' place. We left one hour after we were notified of the situation. The McDowells' place was at least eight miles away. That teen really had to have been scared to run that distance to tell me the story.

I figured that the teen's story must have had some truth. I didn't remember the last time that I had visited the McDowell area. I remembered the old-style mansion that he lived in. I remembered that someone told me that the property had been passed down from generation to generation, and that the house was located deep into the woods. Prior to getting to the house, there used to be an open field to graze cattle. Dusk was upon us, as we reach the outskirts of McDowell's land. We took the long winding trails through the deep canopy of trees. It was an eerie feeling, because there was no visibility. After about a mile, a distant fire illuminated the path. Immediately, my deputy and I pulled out our rifles. The fire intensified as we approached the main housing areas. The smoke loomed all around the wood-line, limiting our visibility. With astonishment I looked around and thought, "What the hell happened out here." Dead cattle littered the ground. My hair stood on the back of my neck seeing this horrific site. Once we reached the edge of the wood line, we could clearly see the origin of the fire. Every building in sight was on fire. I smelled the scent of burning flesh and smoke in the air. The stench of burnt flesh intensified as we moved past the horses' stable. My inner fear of the unknown suddenly took over. We stopped, locked and cocked our weapons. There was something weird going on. Confusion turned into panic, and we didn't take a step further. We stood there paralyzed with horror. The deputy quavering voice asked, "Boss, what if we're being set up for the kill?"

I interrupted his statement, "Close your mouth and keep your finger on the trigger. We'll backtrack to the wood-line, take cover and wait until daybreak to go inside the house."

The fear of the unknown turned into panic, and we both sprinted back into the wood-line. Daybreak was only a half-hour away. Hopefully, my other deputy and the town doctor would catch up with us by then. As I sat there watching the fire burn uncontrollably, I felt that there was something evil happening. In any case, I was satisfied to wait, because whatever happened had already happened. My deputy and I didn't pretend to be scared. There were no words said between the two of us. Our eyes stayed pinned on that ungodly sight. Waiting, watching, for something to erupt. The sun appeared over the horizon in the east, and yet my backup had not shown. I nudged my deputy, who was wide-awake. "Ready," the deputy gave me a pensive look. We mounted our horses this time, and rode towards the house quickly. We dismounted in a hurry, rushed through the mud, and ran to the right side of the front door. We were fully armed with our rifles, ready to fire on anything that moved. The door was already cracked opened, so I pushed the door open with the rifle muzzle. Both of us stood in the doorway in total disbelief. The young lad's story was true.

Death had rained on the McDowell's ranch. Dead bodies lay from door to door. Blood of the dead dripped from the walls. Puddles collected on the floor and drained from the ceiling. This was a monstrous act. In the ten years that I had been a Marshall, I had never seen anything as repulsive as this. My deputy had an eye full, and ran outside and began to vomit. I realized then that whatever had happened there was over, and I was damn glad that I wasn't there to be a part of it. I decided to walk through the house in order to find out what had happened. Two men were shot in the head and one man had been cut in half by a shotgun blast. They must had been playing cards, because the table was still erect and money was laying around the guts of the men. Another man had been draped over the dinner table. His mouth was still stuffed with something. I moved to the back porch. Stretched toward the woodline lie a trail of dead men, spaced far apart from each other. They were all lying on their stomachs. One guy was 20 yards away from the house, another was 30 yards, and then another was 100 yards. All of them had multiple wounds. A carpet of blood started from the steps and ran to the last man. I deducted that these were the ones who tried to make a run for safety. They had been caught by surprise. I asked myself, "What was the motive? Who did this?" The doctor had toured the house and was standing behind me when I was talking to myself.

"Mother of God. That's a damn good question. Did you see the genocide left upstairs?" He asked.

I looked at the doctor and saw that his skin had turned a pale clammy white. I asked him, "you mean there are more dead?" I remembered that blood that was dripping from the ceiling when we first entered McDowell's house. "Was it old man McDowell?" I asked, waiting for anyone to answer.

The doc answered, "I couldn't tell." I was astonished with the answer.

My voice raised an octave, "What in the shit do you mean that you couldn't tell? You're an educated man."

Lips curling with disgust, Doc answered, "A double-barreled shotgun at close range didn't leave much on either of them to see." I felt like a trapdoor had opened in the pit of my stomach. I felt the pangs of internal conflict. I initially felt relieved that someone had done mankind a favor to rid the law-abiding citizens of a scum sucking maggot like McDowell off the face of this earth. I couldn't care less about McDowell, but after speculating and rationalizing about the impact of this massacre, I thought about a range-war. I figured that it was my duty to stop this vendetta before it expanded. Suddenly, my deputy came running my way from the wooded area that led from the swamps. We all ran towards the swamp. I looked at the evidence. It was footprints of a horse and one man.

Angry at the deputy's response, I snapped, "What the fuck do you mean, wasting my time with one set of footprints. We're looking for a lynch-mob, at least 10 to 15 men. Go look some more."

The deputy puzzled, by my response, answered, "Marshall with all due respect, if we get that one man he'll be able to provide us with information." I pointed in direction of the swamp and looked at the sky, seeing that a storm-front was moving our way.

I answered, "You'd have to be a complete idiot to go there. Look at those skies." I knew that whomever was out there wouldn't survive the swamps. Besides, I believe that the immediate danger is gone, and accomplished what they came for. I saw enough death for today.

CHAPTER 3

THE GENESIS OF THE BUFFALO MAN

July 20,1875 (Three years earlier)

Times were hard and life was never fair, but early teaching taught me that adaptation would always be the way of survival.

My Grandfather used to use the analogy about how gazelles adapted with speed, to evade the most ferocious beast in the jungle, the lion. The young, sick, and older gazelles would get eaten. He'd ask me was this feat a measure of adaptability, survival of the fittest, or just luck? I got the feeling that he was trying to explain how the real world would be once I became an adult. Within the month I'd turn 17. In my mind, the crossroads of life were just around the corner. A choice had to be made soon. Most young men ventured in the path of least resistance, which often meant working on somebody's farm as a sharecropper or becoming a servant for the remaining wealthy landowners in the territory. This choice was an easy transition for our elders. After the war, they worked as sharecroppers for their ex-masters. Housing, clothing, and food were provided to them if they decided to take this path. To me that lifestyle always meant, the freedom to be trapped. Entrapped in a society that confined, true freedom. In my mind this also meant freedom without opportunity. I thought about the gazelle analogy. "A gazelle is free to roam the jungle, waiting to be eaten by the lion. Why limit my chances for survival in an area full of lions?" Personally I didn't want to be a sharecropper for the rest of my life. I had a deep feeling that there was a true calling for me out there. I sincerely believed that without opportunity, freedom meant nothing. I made my mind up. I wanted to become a professional soldier. I was still naive about life in general, but I felt that being in the Army would bring me automatic respect, freedom, and the opportunity that I was looking for.

One night before dinner I told my mom that I would be enlisting in for the Army. She stared at me with a smile. She then returned back to preparing dinner for the family. I'm not sure if she took me seriously, but nothing else was said at the dinner table.

Word had passed quickly about my intention. My older brother questioned me about my decision. He looked at me with a sarcastic look, shook his head, and asked, "Why." I'm sure he wasn't looking for a one-word answer. I held my anger back because it was my decision, and I didn't feel compelled to give him an answer. However, he was my big brother and I owed him the respect of being the senior in the house. I paused to collect my thoughts, and said "Well there would be one less mouth to feed, I'd make thirteen dollars instead of three dollars a month. My food, clothing shelter would be free of charge." My brother didn't look convinced with those answers. I then felt compelled to tell him the real truth. "I'm sure military life offers me something better in life. If you're happy doing what you're doing, fine. But I want something different. I want to do something that others can be proud of. I want to be respected. I'm looking for equality, advancement, and opportunity." The words were spoken straight from my heart. My brother could see that I was sincere, but he could also see that I was living a pipe dream. He could see through my lack of wisdom.

My brother shook his head in total disagreement and responded. "A uniform doesn't equal respect, equality and any of that other nonsense that you're talking about. You'd be black man in a white man's uniform, and that's all. The rest is bullshit.

The white men see you just as you are. If you do make it in the Army, you'll be put on some type of work detail. You'll become another insignificant pawn that works for the Government. Anyway, why would you want to kill Indians? The only thing that they want is to have the same opportunity that you're looking for."

With all that my brother said, my mind was made up. I had a vision, and it was my destiny to be and to live as I saw fit. Nothing was said about the Army for a couple of weeks.One morning my parents decided to go into town to pick up corn-flower and sugar. I normally went with them because down town New Orleans was always exciting.

When we reached town I said to my mother, "Mom, let me go." She looked at me with a puzzled look. It's ironic that we stopped the carriage at a crossroad. The choice had to be made then, because my mother knew that my decision was final about enlisting in the Army. She turned around to face me. I could feel the pain in her heart. However, she knew that Army life was better than sharecropping. A nod of approval came with a tear that ran down her cheek. I kissed her and jumped off the carriage. She left me in a trail of dust. I waved good-bye but my mother never looked back. She knew I might not ever return home. I figured that opportunity only knocks on the door of life once. I seized the moment when I saw the opportunity, and I was on my way to new horizons.

It was an extremely hot and humid morning. The sun was in full bloom at about 10 o'clock. There were no clouds in the sky and the air was stagnant. The streets of New Orleans were crowded with masses of people. I was excited to get started on my quest, I kept bumping into people. I was proud of what I was going to become. The whites looked at me as if I didn't belong. I stared back at them thinking, "What the hell are you looking at?"

I reached the enlistment office by mid afternoon. I was in total awe upon my arrival. There was a line of men waiting to enlist. There were four lines spaced 200 meters deep. I got in the last line. The thoughts in my mind ran amuck. I ask myself, "Do these guys have the same dream as I? What were these guys looking for? Where did they all come from?" Most men looked like they came out of the same environment that I left. Some were civil war rubbish that drifted from the ruins. A third of them were old enough to be my grandfather. Two men that were in front of me smelled like whiskey, and looked like boozers or alley scum. There were some that looked like they had traveled a long journey. Those were probably the unlucky ones that were on their last leg. They looked tired as though they were ready for someone to put them out of their misery. Some were carrying their life long valuables on their backs.

There were a few things that we all had in common: the sun was baking us to a crisp. Most of us looked like a bunch of animals. The blacks occupied the last two lines. The white inductees occupied the first two lines of the four columns. The whites were not in any better condition. They looked just as broke. Most of these guys were unshaven and had beards. Their attire was ragged and dirty. Basically they shared the same commonalties as we did. However, I thought some of them looked like criminals that were on the run. Actually it looked as if the prison gates had opened at the enlistment office. There were all types in line waiting to start another life.The lines inched their way slowly inside the small building. The heat and body odor increased as the day wore on. Neither of these obstacles bothered me because I knew what I wanted. The temperature decreased because when evening came. It was my turn to go inside the enlistment office. I stepped inside the small building and I heard a loud but deep voice holler, "Next man." I moved up to the desk where the sergeant was processing paperwork. He was a large dark haired man and wore a handlebar mustache. He had an Irish accent and greeted me differently from the others. I guess he was baffled by my youth.

"Well lad, you want to be a Cavalry soldier?" Not knowing the difference between a Cavalry, Infantryman or any other army type, I answered, "Yes sir."

His eyes widened, and he shouted, "Don't call me sir, I work for a living."

I answered, "Yes." He stood up in his chair and looked down at my small frame and angrily said, "It's Sergeant boy. Sergeant McMahan to you." Terrified at this large bear of a man I just nodded my head. Then he smiled at me. He pulled out the contract that was located in his desk and began to explain what it meant.

"Okay young lad, this is your contract that simply states that you're enlisting in the Cavalry for a period of three years. Can you ride a horse?"

I nodded my head and answered with a studder "Yes Sa ...Sergeant." The Sergeant's voice lowered one octave and attempted to lower my defense to get a sincere response from me. "Do you know what you're getting yourself involved with? A soldier's life is a hard life." We stared at each other for a moment. I think he was waiting for me to change my mind. We made eye contact, and his eyes must had seen and measured my heart. Moments after the sergeant finished his sensitivity sensing parlay he nodded his head, held out his hand and said to me, "Good-luck lad. God be with you. Sign this piece of paper, walk through those double doors, and a officer will be with you shortly to swear you in. Hope we cross trails someday. Take care of yourself."

The room that I walked in was full to maximum capacity. Again the air was stale and reeked with body odor. Another hour passed before anyone showed up to swear us in. Finally a tall slender officer walked in the room. He was clean-shaven and looked well groomed. He glanced around the room for a moment. The room came to a dead silence.

"Gentlemen, I want to be the first to commend you on your choice to become soldiers. Tonight you men will be transported by way of train to Fort Seal Oklahoma. At Fort Seal you will go through basic training for a period of four to six weeks. Once you finish basic training, you will be separated. Some will go to Infantry units, some will go to field hospital units, some will go to field Engineer units & a few will go to our newest unit the 10th Cavalry."

I felt relieved because my quest for something was now in motion. Late that night we began to board cattle cars. Prior to boarding, we were given rations and a full canteen of water. We were packed in the cattle car like sardines. There was just enough room to sit down. Hay lined the floor for cushion. The only way to sleep was to lay back to back with someone. Fortunately, we left late that night, so conversation was limited to snoring. It was hard to sleep because of the tight quarters in the cattle car and the bumpy train ride. Occasionally the train would stop to allow us to stretch our legs. With the extreme temperature in the day and night, spirits remained high. The trip lasted two days. It was about mid-afternoon when the train came to a halt. The door opened and a soldier jumped on board before we had the opportunity to get off. He had average size build, heavy mustache, and a heavy five o'clock shadow. The train car was quiet. He began to talk loudly. He grinned and said, "Good morning girls. Did you enjoy your trip?" The sergeant confused everyone with his politeness. He continued on. "I hope the train ride didn't come as an inconvenience to any of you." He walked around with a smile as if he were inspecting our reactions. He continued walking slowly with a smile. "My name is 1st Sergeant McCish. I want to welcome you to Lawton Oklahoma. Fort Sill is your new home. It also houses some of the most savage Indian tribes in the United States, the Kiowo, and Comanchees." There was a long pause. Like a light switch that turns on, the sergeant's attitude went from a nice politeness, to a raging maniac. His face turned to stone, and his voice raised three octaves. "This god damn train car smells like someone took a shit in it. Well, you want to be soldiers, ah? I'm here to make your life a living hell. If you want to wear my uniform you gotta go through me. I'm gonna separate the men from the boys. There's no room for boys in my army. I know that some of you are thinking that you don't stand a chance because you're black trainees. Well let me put your little minds at ease. You're right, I hate you because you're black. I hate every damn human, to include Mexicans Trash, dam wet backs, white trash, especially the nigger lovers, and now I hate you. Not because you're all black but because you look like shit and smell like a fucking Billy Goat. I believe that you're a waste of good government money. I wasn't asked to train you bunch of monkeys, I was ordered to. You will take all orders from me, and only me. When I say jump, you ask how high sergeant. When I say move you'd better move like the wind. One more thing to put in the back of your little fucking minds. People say that you black trainees will never make good soldiers. They say that the best place for you during this conflict with the Indians is in the cotton-fields and on the farms with all of the other animals. To me I don't give a shit either way. To me personally I think you're all lower than a snake's belly. In 30 seconds I want you off this stinking ass cattle car, lined up in a straight formation, ready to march in the front gates of the Fort." The Sergeant started the countdown, "20, 19," panic set in and everyone scrambled out the door of the boxcar. The countdown continued, "17, 16, 15, get off my god damn car," the Sergeant shouted, "13, 12." Finally the cattle car was clear and everyone was in a straight line. The Sergeant continued to rant, rave, an occasionally kick us around. After the entire demeaning exhibition, we moved out in rout to our new home. We walked for about an hour before we reached the front gates of the Fort. Sergeant McCish was relentless on his assault to make our life true hell. We moved to an open field area equipped with mildewed, weathered tents. My spirit wasn't broken by McCish's attacks, but my enthusiasm began to fade when I saw that my military habitat is a tent. Everything that I expected out of basic training came true to form. The training wasn't difficult. Long hours at the rifle range, hand to hand combat, and close order drills made up the bulk of training. The harsh elements that training was conducted in made life difficult during basic training. Long hours at the rifle range meant long hours of baking in the Oklahoma Desert sun. On a normal day we would lose two to three men from heat exhaustion. There was never enough water, and there was no shade. Long hours in the heat and stupidity had resulted in accidental deaths at the firing range. Private Alvin Taylor, a friend of mine, was firing in the standing position for record fire. It had been extremely hot that day. The first time he fired, he scored sharpshooter. This score wasn't good enough for him. He talked the range sergeant into letting him improve his score. The heat had taken its toll on Taylor. Taylor fainted from the heat, and his weapon dislodged a bullet in the temple of an unsuspecting soldier next to him. The soldier fell to his death. It had been three long weeks in training and we hadn't fought the Indians yet. However, our numbers grew smaller as the days passed. Some died from training accidents. Some simply died from diseases such as tuberculosis, cholera and pneumonia. Heat, poor medical assistance, poor diet, and hard training accounted for one-third of our casualties. My morale remained high because I knew there wasn't anything to go back home to. The morale of the men that had families and loved ones faded. The time spent in the field and the slow paying Quartermaster pay system didn't help either. Desertions began to hit our ranks. With the bad goes the good. The hardships that were imposed on us forced the unit to bond. I wonder if that was part of the plan or just a sign of the times. During the off times, which were few and far between, we played horseshoes and baseball. But, the most famous after hours activity was card playing. This was ironic because everyone was broke. Cliques began to form and new friends were made. My favorite associates were three individuals who were professional soldiers in my mind and unique in their own ways. Their names were Blake (Stone-Head) Jefferson, John (Wildcat) Wade, and Rick (Old Man) Jacobs. Blake was from Memphis Tennessee and 17. He got the name, "Stone Head" from the way his head was shaped. His head was shaped like a perfect square. One day McCish asked Blake a simple question that Blake couldn't answer, so McCish responded angrily, "Is your head full of stones?"

Blake responded, "Apparently so sergeant."

McCish smiled and said, "That's what I like. A man with a set of balls, but stupid enough to give an answer like that. Now give me 100 squat thrust, smartass."

Blake and I were the youngest men in the platoon. Thus, our youth was the common ground that we shared. The biggest difference between us was that Blake was outspoken. He was willing to take an ass whipping just as long as he got his two cents in first. John was from Louisville Kentucky, and was 23. He was called "Wildcat" for a number of reasons. The name wildcat originated from the name "polecat," which was started by our loving Sergeant McCish. One day during an inranks inspection McCish walked by John, who had apparently forgotten to clean himself after taking a field dump. John cut a fart before McCish had finished his platoon inspection. McCish became volatile and began to sniff out the culprit. McCish had a keen sense of smell that pinpointed John's pungent odor.

"We got ourselves a stakin ass pole cat in this platoon," stated the Sergeant. However, later that day a few platoon members started to tease John about smelling like a polecat. John responded like a wild cat by aggressively jumping over the card table and on top of two of our peers. After that incident, John took on the name "Wildcat," because of his aggressive nature. Like Blake and I, John was distant from the platoon, and somehow he gravitated toward our social circle. His presence was advantageous to us, because no one in the platoon screwed with us when John was around. John became our guardian angel.

There were a couple of qualities that I didn't like about John. He had a short fuse, and would openly criticize authority figures. We'd look over that character flaw without question, because we didn't want to become victims of an ass beating. There was one other unique characteristic about John. He was a half-breed. He was half Apache and half Black. His unique heredity characteristic could account for his sort temper and aggressive nature.

Rick's, my other close friend and confidant, home was unknown to us all. It was probably somewhere in the Deep South. He was called the "Old Man," because he was the oldest man in the platoon, and probably in the Regiment. He had to be at least 50 or better. He was wise with his wisdom, and was a veteran of the civil war. Rick was respected by all the Officers and NCOs including Sergeant McCish. He too kept his distance from the platoon's inner social circles. He was a loner. However, we gravitated towards him to provide us with insight. Rick enjoyed his space, but we could always find Rick in the middle of a poker game. It was confusing to me to how someone could be both a gambler and a loner. Rick had a gift of improvisation. Adapting and overcoming any harsh conditions seem to be his mastery. I felt that his knowledge is invaluable to anyone. Most of the time he was pretty rough with me, but he showed empathy for Blake and me in his own way. I often wondered how fate brought us together.

It had been five weeks since we'd started. The basics of becoming a soldier were concluding. Our training was becoming more focused to the type of skills that we needed for becoming Cavalry Soldier. Horseback training, marksmanship training, and saber training dominated the next few weeks of training. Sergeant McCish started to lighten up with his insults.

September 1875

The fall seasons brought cool winds from the north. The desert night breeze was harsh but tolerable. The sun was still relentless during the evening. The wind kicked up just enough dust to be annoying. Sand and dirt covered everything. The food and water always had sand in it. The Indians had to prepare for the winter, which we knew meant that they might leave the confines of the reservations. Settlers had the same idea to expand their horizons, so conflict was inevitable. Herds of cows needed land to graze. Buffalo roamed wild and needed the same. Land mongers would build barbed wire fences that would obstruct the Indian's food chain and way of life. The threat of winter would bring the bitter cold sting of conflict. The signs of war were in place, but no one knew exactly when the reign of terror would begin. The air of uncertainty loomed in the minds of men that lived in that territory. The deadly game of chess began. Finally the training period was over. We transferred from one side of the post to another Tent City on the post. The conditions were deplorable. The only noticeable changes that I could tell, were that we were granted the freedom to roam within the confines of our Tent City, and were also given an increase of rations. Activity or lack of activity had a negative effect on our morale. Idleness, cramped living conditions, poor hygienic conditions, and cold fall nights brought about discipline problems. Fights between soldiers became an every day event. Then there was the complaint that white officers imposed their prejudice and wills on the lower enlisted. Cholera and other diseases unfolded. One soldier died of pneumonia. Rumors ran rapid through out the platoon. Soldiers became restless because we resented the idea of dying without even firing a shot. Finally the unthinkable happened. Four soldiers deserted from our ranks.

Finally our company got orders to deploy. It was like a breath of fresh air. Attitudes changed just like the unpredictable weather. Our orders were to move the whole Regiment out early morning.

That night Lieutenant Jacobs our platoon leader briefed us about the situation. "The San Carlos Reservation Apache braves have currently left the reservation and have stared reigning terror on the settlers within the area. They have raided a coal-mining town located fifteen miles on the outskirts of the reservation. We are going to investigate what happened. We're going to leave tonight as the company's quartering party, and the company will leave at the break of day." It was a two day ride to San Carlos. At about midnight it was quiet except for an occasional conversation between soldiers who were on the quartering party. The anticipation of battle filled the air. The butterflies in my stomach ran amok. The gates opened and we rode out in column formation into the night. At this point I knew that my life would never be the same. We rode through the desert for two days and finally reached the outskirts of town about mid afternoon. The lieutenant instructed my squad to move in first. Rick, the squad leader of my squad saluted the lieutenant lead the squad and cautiously approached town. As we approached the town, we smelled the scent of charred wood. From the outside it looked like the town had tried to defend itself. Windows and doors were boarded, and wagon wheel carts were overturned. The Indian scout that was with us motioned for Rick to stop. We dismounted our horses and stood there motionless, listening. The town was lifeless. It was like a ghost town. We waited at least 15 minutes before we approached the entrance into town. Stone Head Blake looked at Rick with a puzzled look, and questioned him. Rick quickly cut off Blake in mid sentence, "Keep your mouth closed and listen." Rick called for John and I, and then motioned to the Indian scout. We assembled on Rick.

Rick spoke with a faint whisper, "I want you guys to have a look before I bring the squad inside." The small hairs on the back of my neck stood up. The sergeant continued, "Be real careful, keep a sharp eye and keep your fingers on the trigger. If you make contact I'll bring the rest of the squad in to help. The bell tower and the hotel roof seem to be good sniper positions. Once you clear those buildings that over-watch the town John will signal us to come in. Wait a few more minutes before you move, and listen."

John responded, "What the hell are we listening for."

Rick responded like a teacher to a pupil, "You're tuning your ears. If something is in there, and it moves you will hear it." The only distinct noise to be heard was the gusting dry wind. The Indian scout orchestrated our movement through the flank of the town. We entered the church that had the bell tower. We hammered the back door with the butts of our rifles until the door opened. John entered first and I entered next with my rifle in the ready position.

It was a horrible site. I gawked in disbelief. John immediately puked at the abominable picture. The Indian scout that was with us must had been a spiritual man because he immediately pulled out his holy cross as if it had the power to ward off evil spirits. Dead people had been erected in the church seats as if they were at mass. The floor and pews were covered with puddles of blood. Judging by his white blood stained collar the minister had been hog tied to the podium, headless. If the Indians were trying to send a message by displaying their ruthlessness, I understood it loud and clear. If this display of barbarous act was supposed to effect me psychologically, it was working. I was terrified. We were paralyzed with fear, and didn't move another step.

Finally, after John's stomach settled, he cautiously moved up the steps of the bell tower. The scout and I stayed below and waited for John's return. While waiting, the only thought that was running through my mind was, "How evil people can be." This was as evil act. This was the first time that I'd seen death in this fashion. I had seen relatives who had died from a natural death, but nothing of this magnitude. Some of the dead were hacked to death with tomahawks. Others had gapping holes in their chest that were created by blunt objects like spears, and some of the victims' throats were cut from end to end. The bodies had been there for a while because the blood on the floor was drying, and the bodies were stiff as boards. I hated the thought of dying a death like this. Like a girl that lost her virginity, I lost something that day. Moment's later John called out from the bell tower, "All clear." When Rick noticed that we had secured the bell tower, the remainder of the squad moved in. They became thunderstruck at the horrible site. That night we waited for the arrival of the main body. Blake and I had sentry duty together. I noticed when I walked duty that night most of the platoon was awake. I believe most of them felt like me. My nerves were on the edge, I could feel the bile in my stomach, and worried that I would die a violent death.

October 1875

One month had passed and we hadn't picked up a trail of the raiding party. They had simply disappeared into the desert. The only known fact was that they were Apaches. Our Company Indian Scout name was Cactus, a Cheyenne native, demonstrated his excellent tracking skills in our platoon's quest to find these band of savages. One early night after a long day of patrolling Cactus, John, Blake, Rick, and I were sitting around a warm fire engaged in a game of cut throat. I had asked Cactus his opinion about the ghost that we were chasing. The scout looked at me with a skeptical look. He folded up the cards in his hands.

He asked us all as a group, "Are you sure you want to know my opinion?"

Rick answers, "Yeah Cactus tell us." Cactus stood up and pointed towards the vast horizons of mountains that surrounds them. In a shrewd manner, he explained, "They are out there."

He turned in another direction and pointed at another set of mountains, "Or they are out there." Cactus sat down and continued. At that point he had our attention. Those Apaches we're chasing were clever. The reason we didn't pick up their tracks was because they cleverly made tracks that lead in twenty different directions. The reason why we never could find them is because they never went anywhere. They hid and watched every move we made. When we moved, they moved. This band of Apache is ruthless, cunning, and skilled at the art of reigning terror. They were bitter at something and willing to die for their cause. After capturing the town, they had stayed there for days and tortured everyone. They commandeered enough food, water and horses to last them awhile. I believe that the only time that they will come out, is to get more food, water, and horses. These Apaches were dangerous. They didn't give a damn who they hit to get what they need. Their tactics were to sweep up anything in their path, like a tornado, and leaving nothing but devastation. Unfortunately for us, we didn't have to find them, they would find us. In their eyes we were not the hunters, but the prey. In the event that we were captured, we knew to save one bullet for ourselves. Unfortunately little was known about fighting Apaches. Most of the officers in this regiment had little to no experience on any battlefield. Most of the white officers had volunteered for this assignment because it meant a cash bonus and early promotion. That night and after Cactus' explanation, Rick made sure his squad was always prepared for the unknown.

CHAPTER 4
CONFLICTING VIEWPOINTS

It was a cool breezy fall night. The moon illuminated the sky and vast desert terrain. A light haze of fog drifted in from the East. The coyotes cried out. The fires were bright and the Apache war counsel met to discuss upcoming events.

The war paint on each brave face was thick and heavy. The motivational dance of war brought inspiration to the people. The apaches gathered around Chief Nana, waiting for him to start the meeting.

Their situation dictated what had to be done. The time was ripe to send a message to the President of the United States, to say that the Indian nation would no longer recognize the empty treaties. The chief walked in and looked into the eyes of people that he was willing to sacrifice in order to bring Washington to its knees and negotiate a meaningful peace settlement. He took a moment to remember what events led him to defy the government. He remembered how the black plague of degradation had taken its toll in the reservations. The only promise kept by Washington was the land agreement. Yet the old and young were weak with starvation and diseases. The only monthly shipment of beef had ended a year ago. They were given infertile fields that were supposed to yield crops. The chief nephew died from a impetigo related disease that had spawned from the polluted water located on the reservation months ago. The chief's heart beats with wrath of vengeance. He forced back tears of pain and focused on passion to get back what had once belonged to his people. He took advantage of the moment to allow his patriots to bellow the war cry.

The cry for war got louder and louder as the Chief stood and watched his people hoot and howl. The medicine man would cleverly feed the crowd's need for reinforcements by throwing ignighter on the warming fires, which made the fire illuminate brighter and brighter. Chief Nana picked up a rifle with one hand and a spear with the other, and raised them high so that every one could see him. His painted face meant war. The rifle and spear signified the weapons that would be used to kill the enemy. The raising of the arms meant that it was time for his speech. The howling and drum beating became silenced. Nana said, "Remember my words of iron. Time and time again a piece of paper had been signed by Washington and our Brothers that was supposed to insure that we live in peace and prosperity, and improve our way of life on the reservations. Every day, every minute and every second that passes, these empty promises are broken by the white man. There is no respect for our way of life, and there never will be respect. The white man wants to confine us to a piece of worthless land called a reservation, so we can live by his rules. We tried to exist by his rules, but we suffered and died by his gains." The Chief paused. His face hardened, veins surfaced in his neck, his eyes bulged from their sockets, his mouth contorted grotesquely. He changed from a composed warrior chief to a neurotic, obsessed warmonger. He went on, "Our words of peace will be spoken with these weapons that I hold up in front of you. Kill the enemy; continue to take back what the white man has stolen from us. We will take back the land that our forefathers lived on and passed on to us, so that we may some-day pass it on to our children. Kill the enemy, so that we will have fertile soil to grow our crops, allow our cattle to graze and feed our families. Kill the enemy, so that we may hunt wherever we desire and fish in any pond or lake that we choose. This spear that I hold in my hand signifies for you to plunge your spears in the corrupt hearts of the white devils. Then and only then our true message of peace will be heard." The crowd of warriors was aroused by Nana's words of iron and erupted into a crazed frenzy of yells and chest beating. Again the chief dampened the excited crowd by raising his arms to conclude his speech. "Once again Washington is desperate to talk peace. They send troops after us. They sent dark-skinned bluecoats after us. That's an insult. They sent inferior bluecoats to humiliate our cause. These dark-skinned bluecoats used to be slaves. They too should be defiant against Washington. They will die a double death for siding with the white men. Slaughter the slave soldiers. This will send a message to Washington about putting inferior troops against our braves. I believe that we will break their will to fight after the first blow of conflict." Nana spoke with arrogance and confidence. For the remainder of the night, the tribal council talked over strategy and tactics while the tribe indulged themselves with spirit water and celebration. Everyone was confident in the upcoming events. They had already assured themselves a victory.

CHAPTER 5

DESTINY OF WILLS

Later that night, the company column had caught up with our platoon. I was glad to see them. The war drums of the Apaches had been beating all night long. Our company had over-extended itself, too far away from the regiment coverage. If there were a fight, our regiment wouldn't be able to help. The apaches knew of this ambitious tactical screw-up. The officers tried to cover up their blunder but all the subordinates knew. Our company column quickly moved out at dawn. The idea was to backtrack back to Regiment's area of operation. The company moved at a rapid pace through the open terrain of the desert. We slowed to a snail's pace as we made our way through a thinly vegetated ravine. Our platoon was the lead platoon for the company, and Rick's squad was the lead squad for the platoon. Therefore, I had first hand knowledge of what we were up against. Our cautious movements through this ravine brought anxiety to everyone's mind. Cactus and the other scouts, at the extreme front edge of the company stopped. The Company stopped its movement. We were in a bad position to stop because high ground surrounded us. Suddenly hell broke lose. Shots were fired from all directions. The man that was next to me head exploded. The man's flesh and blood splattered all over me. The horses were disturbed by the sudden gunfire, it became difficult to settle them down. It was hard to figure out where the gun fire was coming from. It was total chaos. The sniper's puffs of smoke surrounded us. A command came to dismount the horses. We dismounted and took cover behind whatever was available. The sniper fire suddenly ended. The only sound was the crying of our horses. The next orders we heard were to dig in. I knew then that the fight was on. The horses were moved to the middle of the defensive formation. Like desperate moles we began to dig in the earth fast and hard. Suddenly I saw Cactus and the other scouts running back towards us screaming, "Here they come." To our front just below the horizon clouds of dust could be seen. There must have been over 100 braves attacking. They were conducting a straight frontal assault. Parts of the second platoon moved to our right flanks to reinforce our position. They started to dig in frantically. Rick was next to me. He felt compelled to remind me, "Remember kid, you better fight like there's no tomorrow. These guys don't take prisoners." The large body of warriors closed the gap 250 to 300 meters. My heart began to pump harder and my fingers trembles against the rifle trigger. Within seconds they closed the gap within 100 meters. I wanted to shoot but the order to fire hadn't been given yet. They were so close that I could see the war paint designs on their faces. Finally the magic order came. **Fire!** We fired a thunderous volley of bullets directly into the charging frontal ranks. Horses, and Indians came tumbling to the ground, throwing dirt and dust in all directions. The second platoon that was on our right flack hadn't fired yet. As we reloaded I heard the second platoon order. "Fire!" The 2nd platoon had the same results as us. But, the momentum of the Indian's attack was so fast the volleys had little effect. The next orders were to fire at will. By the time I reloaded my weapon, the thrust of the assault had penetrated our defense. Horses and braves came poring into our ranks. Hand to hand fighting broke out. Braves charged into our ranks, running over whomever was in their way. Apaches spears plunged into the bodies of some of our men. Point blank range firing hit whatever was near. I looked around quickly and saw an Apache charging in my direction. I swung around with the butt of rifle and hit him in the face. I hit him with such force the rifle butt broke. I quickly pulled out my revolver, and shot another Apache in the back who had wrestled Rick to the ground. Close order fighting continued until the 3rd platoon charged in to reinforce our platoon. Finally the Apaches broke off their attack and retreated back. They lost many in trying to retreat. I looked around at the devastation. Men, Apaches, and horses covered the ground, bleeding. Puddles and streams of blood flowed throughout our defense. The wounded cried out for help. People scrambled about, recovering ammunition off the dead. The company surgeon and aidmen scrambled around assisting the wounded. I took some ammunition off of two dead men and stuffed their revolvers in my pistol belt. Suddenly shots rang out from a distance. Two soldiers fell prey to Apache snipers. Everyone hit the ground.

Someone cried out, "Did anyone see where it came from?"

Cactus said, "I saw the puff of smoke, then I heard the shot."

Rick yelled, "Yeah the man's body fell before we heard the shot." Rick concluded, "Shit they are probably out of our range."

Apache snipers surrounded us. Sometime during the battle the snipers that we ran into earlier moved to a better vantage point. They could see our every move. We could not see them. We were trapped and pinned down. New orders were relayed from man to man, "Stay low. We move out tonight."

The evening brought extreme temperatures. The sun bore on my backsides and legs. I started to cramp. It was an ugly situation. We were surrounded from all sides by Apache marksmen. A few of the Apache snipers were out of range. The arrogant Apache snipers would expose themselves as if they were at a turkey shoot. They figured that a bunch of untrained soldiers like us couldn't hit the broad side of a barn.

We could see the puff of smoke first, then hear the sound of the shot, and then the dull sounding thud that meant that someone had been hit. Sometimes the bullet would ricochet against a rock causing it to splinter wound an unfortunate victim. A few men died bleeding to death from a rock wound.

As time passed the arrogant snipers inched their way closer to our position. Things were getting desperate. The closer they got the better their accuracy became. An hour had passed and the heat of the desert was taking its toll. Dehydration was setting in, but the canteens of water were with the horses. No one in their right mind wanted to expose himself to hostile sniper fire.

John and Cactus were in front of me and were angry at our leader's inability to make a decision to do something. Suddenly I saw two soldiers to my rear make a rush for the water. The snipers quickly exposed themselves to engage the thirsty soldiers. Abruptly John took aim and engaged and shot at the Apache sniper. John hit his target dead center in the chest. The warrior left a blood trail as he tumbled down the jagged rock cliff. This event sparked confidence in the platoons. All the soldiers that had their Sharps rifles on them started to engage targets. The overconfident Apaches were too close and the exposed ones were killed. At least eight Apaches tumbled to their death. Buffalo snipers hammered a few more Apache warriors that were trying to move out of range. The score was even, but the Apache remained in control of the high ground. The sun was finally setting. Rick crawled over to my position.

"How you looking on ammo, kid?" Rick asked me.

I replied, "Packing plenty, Sergeant."

"Look kid," he said, "Tonight be prepared to win or die. Those Apaches' plan is to keep use trapped in this shit hole. We are caught in a trap and they know it. You know kid, so far we've won two out of two battles, and that's not bad for a bunch of dumb ass niggers. Those Apaches aren't stupid. They know that we cannot last forever in this ravine. I'm sure they also know that a much larger force will come looking for us soon. So I believe that when they hit us this time they'll hit us with everything except for your granny's underwear. It's become a matter of pride." I looked at Rick with a mystified look.

"Damn kid. You're dense as a rock. They were banking that this fight wouldn't last this long. Can't you read between the lines? Remember how they tried to conduct a frontal assault? They figured that we'd run. Remember how their snipers foolishly walked right into range of our rifles? The Apaches think that we're a bunch of dumb niggers, dressed in a white man's uniform. That's why when they attack again, it will be for all the marbles. If they lose this time many of their leaders will lose face. It's not a question of death to them, it's a matter of principle."

I thought about what Rick said and responded, "What happens if we lose, Sergeant?" Rick paused for a moment to collect his thoughts.

He answered, "It all depends who looks at what's lost. The Apaches have learned a lesson, and will not ever underestimate black soldiers again. The white Generals will probably say, What could you expect out of a bunch of niggers? And most of the black unit will dig ditches from now until hell freezes over. Our parents, brothers, sister, and kin will look at it as a tragedy. Historian and newspapers won't hear about it all. We won't view it as nothing, because we'll be dead. So you better fight like there's no tomorrow."

"Damn Rick. You got any good news to tell me," I asked him. Rick smiled and handed me, a pretty pearled handled Bouy Knife.

"Those Spensor Rifles aren't very good at close range. There's usually no time to reload your pistol in the heat of the battle. This knife will help to give you an edge. Remember this when things get ugly. When you think that you're not going to make it, then it's time to get mean. I'm talking about downright honorary stinkin nasty. There will be no second chance, just death. There will be no funeral. The worms and buzzards will have a field day on your corpse."

"That's enough, you're scaring the hell out of me," I said.

"Good. Let what I told you sink in, because that's the way it will be if you lose," he told me. I immediately scratched a few more inches of dirt out from under me for added cover. It was beyond dusk. The overcast skies covered the illumination of the moon. I had never seen it so dark out in the desert before. The movement orders came around. Just as I stood up to move towards my horse gunfire erupted. Quickly, everyone moved back into their futile fighting positions. No one returned fire because nothing could be seen at any distance. Our eyesight had not totally adjusted from daylight to pitch black.

Whatever was gonna happen, was going to happen in the next few minutes. The volume of hostile fire increased, by now we could see the muzzle flash. Judging by the flash the Apaches were only a couple hundred yards away. The Apaches were attacking by foot. And this time they were conducting an infantry fire and maneuver movements. The accuracy of their weapons were limited. However, bullets zinged all around our position. Occasionally a soldier would fall from a hit, but we had not opened fire yet. The muzzle flashes got brighter as they inched their way closer to our position. At about 75 yards we opened fire.

Suddenly, to my rear I could hear the 3rd platoon engaging target. The Apaches had made their way behind us. They were attacking from the rear. Then I heard a thundering herd of horses on our left flank moving in our direction. In response to this movement I saw the 2nd platoon move to reposition themselves to engage the Apache Cavalry. Those sneaky bastards were conducting a three-prong attack. It would be difficult to figure out the direction of the main attack. The Apache had accomplished what they were trying to achieve. Our company was fixed and isolated from supporting each other. Our clear fields of fire were bound by the darkness.

Somehow I remained poised and ready to react. I felt that we were staring death right in the face. But somehow I felt resolved, and was prepared to die that day. My mouth was dry and my trigger finger was trembling. I could hear the pattering of feet to my front. They were closer than I had expected. Rick and I jumped up into a standing position firing at the closest shadows. This action prompted our whole platoon to stand up and fight. Shadows were beginning to fall on the ground. Suddenly the shadows appeared at close range. The masses of Apache warriors retaliated our gunfire volley in exchange with arrows, spears, and Apache rifle fire. Both volleys at close range resulted in a few fatalities on both sides. The Apaches kept charging in to our front. The intensity of fire increased. There was no time for reloading.

Rick looked around at the squad with a crazed look. He pulled out his pistol. The screaming Apaches were sprinting like a thundering herd of buffalos, charging in our direction. I wasn't sure if it was the passion to kill or desperation, but I heard Rick shout out with that same crazed look, "What's the matter you dumb asses? You want to live forever? Today is a fine day to die. Get your lazy asses up. Let's show these assholes what it all about." Rick's words of fire sparked an emotional uproar in the hearts of all of us. Suddenly the mighty word lit the torch, "COME ON!" We became animals and without hesitation sprinted to greet the charging Apache. I was caught up in the moment. There was no fear of death. The only sensation that I had was the need to kill. This fight would be a fight of wills. The massive charging bodies collided.

The initial front ranks men were knocked off their feet by the monumental force of the collision. I was knocked off my feet, and rolled to the right. I raised up the barrel of my sharps rifle and fired directly into the face of an oncoming warrior. The fighting was so close that one could fire in any direction and hit something or someone. The clinching of fists and gnashing of teeth can't describe the intensity of this fight. Nose to nose, toes to toes, strictly hand to hand, and an occasional rifle blast best describes this insane moment. Tomahawks, rifle butts, knives, rocks, dirt, or anything else were fair game to use. I used the remainder of my pistol rounds, so I used my pistol butt as a club.

Like an uncaged killer, I held my pistol/club in one hand and my buoy knife in the other. I swung, clubbed, and jabbed, striking and hitting any Apache in my way. An Apache jumped me from the back and tried to break my neck. I quickly bent at the waist, flipping the brave to the ground. He jumped up and rushed me, knocking us both to the ground. I jabbed my blade deep into his chest. Blood splattered in every direction. I tried to pull the knife out of his chest, but the knife was wedged between his rib cage.

I reached down to pick up my pistol. Another Apache kicked me squarely in the face. I fell directly on my back and hit my head on a rock. I was dazed and couldn't move. The brave grabbed me by my throat and began to choke the life out of me. I couldn't breathe or move. Just as I was about to lose consciousness, the brave screamed loudly from the blade of John. The point of his blade penetrated from his throat and exited his chest. I was still trying to gain consciousness and my breath back. Suddenly members of the 3rd platoon joined the fight. Organized volleys of fire came from the direction of the 2nd platoon. Apparently, the rear and flanking Apache attacks were faint attacks. The main Apache attack was the frontal attack and it had stalled inside the circle of the defense. Now the circle was collapsing and tightening its grip on the main Apache attack. Again the Apaches were caught in crossfire. The momentum of the fight shifted to our company. The organized Apaches' fight turned into a route. They tried to break contact in a organized manner. But, we cut their escape route off everywhere they turned. Over sixty Apaches died in this futile attack. This was a costly scrimmage. In our 33 man platoon, only 6 survived. Second platoon lost 9 men and third lost 5 men. A total of 41 men died in the battle.

I heard a faint voice calling my name. "Mack....Mack... Mack."

John yelled at me while assisting a fallen comrade, "Mack get your ass over here." I frantically ran over to help John.

My heart sank as I identified the fallen companion. Rick had a gaping hole in his abdomen. Puddles of blood were beginning to form as he lay there. John stuffed cloth in Rick's wound and tried to apply pressure. I tried to help John by applying pressure to Rick's wound but the blood flowed out of another exit wound. It was hard for me to believe that a man that had fought in countless major Civil War campaigns was dying there from a minor conflict. Rick's last words were spoken in a lifeless monotone pitch, "It's cold out here. Gotta get some sleep. I'm finally going home." Seconds later, Rick died on the battlefield in the desert.

CHAPTER 6
JUSTICE FOR ALL?

Meanwhile, back in the Apache assembly position Chief Nana called for an emergency war council meeting. Many of the council members were not present because they'd been killed. Nana realized that the momentum they had gained during the previous raids had taken a heavy toll on their warriors. He also realized that his Apache families might starve during the winter months because many of the braves had been killed. He was no longer willing to accept more casualties in exchange for his contempt of the white man.

Prior to this fight, his people felt that they were in control of their own destiny. The Chief and the defunct war council felt that they would send a message to Washington by easily defeating the soldiers of the 9th Cavalry. His vision of victory turned into a nightmare of grief.

The once proud Chieftain addresses his warriors and the war council with a different tone of voice. "Instead of attacking we must fade away into the darkness. We can't afford to lose more lives. Our blood flows deep in the stream of desert sand out there. The dark skinned bluecoats will pay dearly someday for this day. We owe it to our brothers. The dark skinned Buffalo soldiers fought honorably, but the day of revenge is coming. However, for now we must go back to our families on the reservation and prepare for the winter." The chief wiped the war paint from his face, and broke camp. The Apache tribe left, never to return on the battlefield again for a long time. Back at our battle position, the aftermath activity was frantic. Orders came down that we were to move within the next 5 minutes. I was pissed off because there was no time to bury the dead. I felt that this was a direct insult those who had lost their lives for our senior leadership blunders.

After a hard three day ride, we made it back to Fort Hood. We were reorganized, and the remaining six soldiers of our platoon rolled into the 2nd platoon. Green replacements were fed to our company. No one considered John, Blake, or I to be squad leaders. The new squad leader came intact with the green replacements. We all resented that decision but we lived with it. That evening there was a Regimental awards ceremony. The officer senior leadership were awarded medals of valor. Not one enlisted member from our platoon was awarded a medal or citation. Some were awarded medals that didn't directly partici-pate in our battle. My calling to be a soldier was fading with every announcement. Our Captain was promoted to Major for his blunder. Our set of officers in our company were moved to staff positions, and replaced with new ones. I heard John say in a low monotone voice, "Out go the old fools, and in comes the new idiots."

Later that night our new Captain announced to the com-pany that we would be back in the field within four days. He said that our previous mission wasn't complete until we personally escorted the Indians back to the reservation and eliminate the resistance. I thought, *What an idiot. What resistance?* On the third day in garrison I volunteered to assist the Quartermaster Captain to pick up supplies for the post. I did this because I was bored with garrison life. I also thought this would be a great opportunity to visit a town as a soldier. I wanted to feel the acceptance of being special. After all, my desire for respect and recognition was a major reason for my joining the Army. Late that same day, our wagons rolled into town, followed by two squads in a column file formation. I was located in the front of the column because I was carrying the company colors. Judging by the initial response of the civilians, one would think that we were on display in a parade. The people immediately stopped in their tracks to observe our movement through the streets. At this point I felt that that we finally were receiving the proper recognition that we had earned. They stared in awe with their jaws dropped. Some began to point. To this day I still have that false idea of respect and recognition embedded in my mind. We stopped and dismounted in front of the door of the General store. As the Captain and I began to walk towards the door, the owner of the store ran out to greet us. I looked at the storefront window and saw that someone posted the "closed" sign. The owner and the Captain had a few things to discuss alone, but I could hear their conversation.

I listened "Look here Captain, niggers aren't allowed in my store," the owner said.

The Captain responds, "These nigger troops are here to get supplies for the Fort." The Captain pulled out a wad of money and handed it to the owner. "Okay Captain. Have your men to pull the wagons around back and load them in the alley. But remember, no niggers inside." His comments triggered an internal madness within me. Matters began to deteriorate. A group of intoxicated men wandered from the saloon in the direction of our wagons. They started to insult us and called us foul names. This mockery of justice sparked the town people to join in with this sick form of entertainment. I felt helpless because we were under strict rules not to retaliate in the event that something like this happened. Once again I had been mislead about people's attitudes. My disgust reached its peak when I saw the town sheriff join in with the laughter.

Finally the time came to move back out to the field. The temperature dropped to the low thirties and the snow fell and accumulated within minutes. The Northerly wind blew the snow-flakes in every direction.

Once again we moved out on the Great Plains of the desert to pick up the trail of the Apaches that had left the reservation. For three days and two cold nights the elements were relentless in making this job miserable for everyone. Finally, Cactus brought back information on the whereabouts of the Apaches. An hour later we had surrounded the village of teepees. There were no Apache sentries or activity within the camp. The teepees held people whom were just trying to stay warm from the harsh elements. Our foolish Captain made us attack the defenseless village. Mainly women and children were found there. We torched their village and escorted them to the nearest reservation. It was a two-day venture before we reached the reservation. Some of the Apaches had died from the bitter cold. The conditions on the reservation were deplorable. The reservation liaison came out of his warm log cabin to meet with our Captain. The Captain went inside with the liaison to discuss the situation. We pitched camp that night there and allowed the Apache civilians to warm up with us. Most of them were sick and exhausted from the trip. I offered my blanket to a woman and her sick child. Cactus who had been on a tour of the reservation earlier, came over to talk to John, Blake and I by the fire.

"We got the wrong Apaches," Cactus stated. "These Apaches weren't the ones responsible for attacking that town or us. But our leader is planning to arrest the braves that are here. The people at this reservation are starving. There's no food and the lakes are frozen solid. The children are dying from starvation. The last meat shipment here was full of maggots. This reservation land is not capable of harvesting vegetables. This is a bad situation and there's nothing that anyone can do."

I felt compelled to say, "You know, after all is said and done, that idiot Captain will get a medal of valor for escorting a bunch defenseless Apache women back to the reservation." We all agreed and shook our heads in disgust. Three days later after completing that political mission, we walked back through the gates of Fort Sill with innocent prisoners in tow. The situation that I predicted came true. Our Captain was awarded a Bronze Star for bringing the Apaches' uprising to an end. The twelve Apache braves that were brought back were hung without a court hearing. I was appalled at this situation, and hated all the officers that I came in contact with. John had a terrible distrust for authority and would sometimes openly defy their positions. I constantly would have to conduct a self-evaluation of my decision to join the Army. I felt trapped because my contract seemed to go on for an eternity. The cold winter season had come to an end. The desert flowers bloomed. The mountain that surrounded the desert floor brought beautiful color to the desolate Fort. For now our missions changed from fighting to escorting and guarding. Our unit was responsible for escorting stagecoaches from town to town. We occasionally escorted the U.S. Mail. We would sometimes patrol the railroad lines and communication lines within the state.

We were at the disposal of the Governor instead of the president. Our unit had reached a low point. The Governor's inability to manage the military brought contempt and misappropriation of government assets. Our defense postures weakened, and we ended up with ditch digging type missions for the wealthy.

Finally, the inevitable happened. Our platoon was conducting a peacekeeping mission at the local Apache reservation. The platoon's patrol base was in the vicinity of the reservation liaison office. At the time John and I had the responsibility of delivering the mail back to the post that day. Our Lieutenant, a 24-year-old new graduate from West Point, took a squad patrol inside the reservation to inspect the conditions. A few of the brothers and friends of the innocent Apaches that had hung had been planning their escape off of the reservation. They were waiting for the right time and right opportunity.

Blake had been promoted to squad leader. We warned the Lieutenant about the potential outbreak. The Lieutenant figured that he could capitalize on this situation, which would automatically elevate his promotional status. The Lieutenant told Cactus to ride back to the patrol base for reinforcements, and then ride back to Fort Sill to alert the Captain of this explosive situation. The Lieutenant ambitiously approached the group of warriors that were huddled around a warming fire. Without hesitation, five of the Apache warriors pulled out machetes and hacked away at the Lieutenant. He was dead before he hit the ground. Blake and the squad were shocked as they witnessed the Apaches cut away the Lieutenant. By the time they pulled their weapons, they too became victims of the massacre. Ten to twelve warriors left the reservation immediately. John and I ran into Cactus as he was making his way to the to the Fort. He told us what had happened, and we decided to ride to the liaison office first, but we had gotten there too late. The warriors had left a horrifying message. The liaison officer had been hung and degutted like a fish. Blake had been beheaded. His head was stuffed inside of his chest cavity. Blood covered the front porch. John and I had lost another close friend. We immediately rode to the patrol base and told the remainder of the squad to wait for the company. John and I were going to pick up the trail of the escapees. We knew that wouldn't be hard to pick up their trail because their tracks were fresh.

There was no time for anger, or grief. It was time to react. If we waited we'd never be able to pick up their tracks. We searched the immediate area for an hour. This area was a maze of undergrowth, briar bushes and a heavily wooded area. John and I decided to take a break out in the open terrain. We dismounted our horses and stretched. We were both covered with trail dust and mud. John began to pull the briar stickers from his clothing. I had stomach pains from that disgusting site at the liaison office. I took off my boots to allow my feet to air out. I looked back at John, and saw him intensely looking over his horses back and pulling out his Spensor rifle. I glanced in the direction that John was looking.

The search was over. The braves had found us. At about four to five hundred yards away the braves were keeping a comfortable distance away from us, because they thought it was a trap. If we ran, they would have figured out that we were alone without support. I quickly put on my boots and looked at the braves once again. They were not riding in our direction. In fact they were content in watching our every moves.

John whispered to me "At the count of three we'll go for our horses and get the hell out of here." The stare down continued.

"Don't want to get gutted like a fish," I said to John. The distant Apaches started to inch their way forward towards us.

John said, "This will make you shit in your britches. There's about ten of those bastards."

I looked at John and said, "I thought there were twelve of them at first."

John responded, "There were twelve."

John yelled, "Three."

We quickly jumped on our horses and rode in the opposite direction. The braves bolted after us. Our hand-me-down horses were no match for their Apache fleet of foot stallions. Our horses lacked stamina. We knew that eventually the Apache would catch up with us. The Apaches inched their way closer and closer as we made our way into the wood line. We finally made it to the base of the hill. Our horses were exhausted. They were panting and salivating heavily. I looked back at the advancing Indians. They were at least a quarter of a mile away.

"We stand a better chance by way of foot through the wooded areas," John said to me. We grabbed our rifles and water and took off at a moderate pace. I turned again to get a glance at the Apache. They suddenly disappeared out of sight. We started to move up the forward slope of the hill. We forced our way through the dense vegetation and slithered through the mud. After running a quarter of a mile, we began to get winded, and stopped to get our breath.

Suddenly, from out of nowhere an Apache brave stumbled upon us. We were all shocked. We both jumped on him. He tried to evade us, but I tackled him. Both of us fell face first into the mud. John pulled out his knife and plunged it into the back of the brave. I held his head in the mud so he couldn't scream. John plunged the knife two more times in his back for added measures, shouting, "And this one is for Blake you bastard." I didn't think about this brutal act until John pulled the blood-dripping knife out of his back. Johns looked insane and said, "He's probably one of the their trackers. He was the hound dog for the others. We got to move now because he must had been leading others." Three other warriors ran right into us. One brave flew through the air and knocked me off my feet, knocking my rifle out of my hand. I quickly rolled back onto my feet and started swinging with clenched fist. I hit him with a quick blow to the groin and a right heymaker to the jaw, knocking him into a daze. The other Apache bolted at me knocking me off balance. However, by that time I had drawn my buoy knife. He lunged at me once more and my buoy knife caught him in his throat. Meanwhile John was choking the life out another brave with his bare hands. I looked around for the other brave that I dazed. He was gone.

"Ok John that poor son of a bitch is dead," I said. John looked at me with eyes deepened with rage.

"He's not dead enough for me," John angrily said.

"One got away." I said, concerned for our survival. John threw the limp corpse to the ground, and with a new focus said, "Shit. We got to get that son of a bitch because he's on the way to warn the others." We took off in the direction that we thought the brave might have traveled. We started to go back down hill.

John picked up his trail somehow. I had never realized that John was proficient in the art of tracking. It was amazing to see John at work. We'd run, stop, and look for the intricate key that put us a step closer to the escapee. We did this unorthodox type of tracking for an hour. It seemed like we were circling the same area. We'd go uphill and then, downhill. Finally, we were close to our original starting point where we fought and killed those braves. John immediately stopped me. We crouched down in the wood line behind some bushes. "What the hell are we doing?" I asked. "That Apache has probably already warned his brothers."

John looked at me and replied, "That's a smart Apache we are following. It's an old Apache trick. He never went anywhere. He just made a complete circle. He'll be back to check on the dead." I looked at John, shaking my head in disbelief.

"Man, you been hanging around Cactus too long. Have you been eating those peyote buttons again?" I asked him. We watched the immediate area for ten minutes. John was right, that Apache that I decked cautiously approached the dead Apache warriors. The brave walked in front of our position and leaned down in front of the corpses. By the time I looked back in John's direction, he had already drawn his knife and bolted toward the unsuspecting brave. The young brave was dead before he knew what hit him. John pulled his knife out of the dead warrior and wiped the blood off his blade onto the grass. I approach him and we looked at each other for a second. John's eyes had a gray tint illuminating them.

"What now?" I asked John.

John replied, "What do you mean what now?" as he continued to clean his knife off. "We're gonna finish the job."

"Finish what job?"

"Kill the rest of them."

I looked at John and gave scowled, "John you've got to be out your fuckin mind to take on the rest of those son of a bitches.

Count me out of this one."

"Mack, allow that small mind of yours to think for a moment," he said. "If we try to escape, they'll eventually hunt us down until they find us and we don't have horses. We have the element of surprise on our side. Anyway, if we don't kill these braves, other innocent Apaches will suffer in the hands of our idiot Captain." I was wrong about John's heart. I thought that John had become an empty shell. But now he demonstrated a true direction of logic. We cautiously moved through the wood-line for two hours. I'm not sure if it was just luck or fate. I had mixed emotions about finding the remaining eight warriors.

When we found them they were all huddled around a campfire smoking what smelled like wild tobacco. We moved around them until we found the best available vantage point. Like wild lions we stalked their every move, waiting for the right moment to close in for the kill. Dark clouds covered the sky and the rain came pouring down from the heavens. Thunder and lightning followed. We inched our way closer to the braves. John pointed our horses out to me. The rain continued to increase. The thunder sounded like cannons firing. I thought that maybe this weather was symbolic of the future. I quickly gathered my nerves and thought about the task at hand. We crawled back deep into the wood line to establish a plan.

"Ok John. What are we gonna do?"

He answered, "Well Mack, this will be our moment of glory or death. We'll work our way back through the wood line to their blindside, which is about 50 to 75 yards away from their position." John stood up and pointed, "Get up here where you can see what I'm pointing at."

I stood up at looked in the direction. "You see Mack. That patch of bushes right behind those Apaches on the left. That will be our position." I interrupted John as he was trying to explain.

"Our position on the left to do what?"

John answered sarcastically, "What part of the word 'kill' do you not understand Mack? It's time to kill or be killed Mack." I was disturbed with John's decision to risk our lives on what was probably a futile effort to save the innocent. I thought his courage was noteworthy but I knew that taking on eight men was an insane act.

"John," I persisted, "there's eight pissed off, wet, cold, and stoned Apaches out there probably trying to figure out the best way to kill us. You saw what they did to Blake."

Angered by my resistance, John responded, "Look Mack, if you want to sit here like a little bitch and wait to be slaughtered by these savages like some damn goat, then stay. I'm gonna do this with your help or without your help. The choice is yours. So choose now." I knobbed my head reluctantly. John continued with his plan. "Like I said, we'll pop out from behind our hiding positions and close the distance as fast as we can. They shouldn't pickup the noise, because the rain on the wet ground should muffle the noise. We'll shoot on the run because that means the closer we get, the more accurate we get. There will be no time to reload so make every shot count. If you miss, keep going. Our secondary targets are the horses. If by chance the plan goes to shit, make a run for the horses. Hopefully we'll surprise them enough that they will stray from the horses."

We were soaked because the rain was coming down in sheets. Large puddles of water and mud began to form. John, confident of his plan, said, "Mack, we've got to hurry before this rain ends." We quickly moved into position. John was to the right of me. The Apaches were huddled in a circle. John fined-tuned his plan, "I'll take the ones from the 9 to 3 position. You take the ones from the 3 to 9 positions. That way we don't shoot at the same one twice. Try not to fire until we're right on top of them." John grabbed my arm and said, "Make every shot count." We intensely observed the Apaches that were sitting there around the smothered out campfire. The smoke from the campfire was drifting, but the rain was quickly diminishing the smoke's cover.We both pulled out our colt 44s. My heart felt heavy and was beating in my throat. My mouth was dry, and I felt adrenaline rushes with every passing second. The grand finale had come. We jumped out of the wood line quickly. That 50 yards between us looked longer than I had anticipated. Forty and closing. The Apaches didn't notice the splashing of the rain water puddles. I pulled the hammer back on my 44, and closed the distance 20 yards. After a few more steps, hell broke lose. The braves turned around in amazement. They woke up from a dead sleep. I fired one round into one brave, cocked the hammer back and shot another one in the chest. John, who had a slight lead on me, was already at point blank range. He shot one brave in the face, spattering blood and brain matter in every direction. I heard his distant shot again and another brave fell to the ground. Suddenly, one brave tackled me while the other ran for the horses. He wrestled me, and made me prematurely fire my pistol in the direction of the horses. The bullet pierced the horse's neck, killing him, which sent a chain reaction of screaming, panicking horses stampeding into the woods. The warrior's strength was too great. I could fell his overwhelming power taking my weapon from me. I quickly pulled out my buoy knife with my free hand and plunged it into his stomach. He curled over in pain, and I knew he would bleed to death.

John had better results than I. He killed all four of his assigned targets. One of mine escaped.

The scrimmage ended as quickly as it started. Seven Apaches lie dead at our feet, and one escaped death never to return. Once again our will to win gave us an advantage over the numbers. In any case I felt lucky that we lived through this ordeal. We had avenged the death of our fallen best friend, Blake.

Three days after returning back to our base camp in the vicinity of Fort Sill, the day for recognition came once more. The

Commanding General came out to conduct inspections and presented awards. It was a spit and polish event. I was proud that our unit won a battle citation, but the individual awards were appalling. As I anticipated, and regretfully so, our Captain was awarded another bravery medal for stopping the so-called uprising. Once again John and I were cheated. I heard John mumble in ranks while the Captain was getting his medal pinned on by the CG, "That asshole was nowhere to be found." I stood there at attention in deep thought thinking about the past events. I had to ask myself who was really the good guy and who was the bad guy. Was it the proud Apache who was trying to take back the land that they once owned? Was it right that our government had us impose its will onto another culture? It seemed ironic that the Apaches we killed three days ago were trying to get payback for the injustice caused by our faulty judicial process. And now this fool of a Captain was getting an award that John and I fought and killed for. I thought about how the Quarter Master paid a bribe to the store owner, and how the civilians treated us. The next day John and I got sloppy drunk. Our attitude and passion to be soldiers were diminishing by every passing moment.

CHAPTER 7

END OF A NEW BEGINNING

One full year in the service had passed. I was now the legal age of 18. I knew that I was getting older because the hair on my face grew much faster. I grew a mustache to make myself look older. Army activity had been rather dull. The Governor of the state had full control over our activity. One of the big news item was that the 10th Cavalry had captured Victoria. It was a good feeling to know black units would have their place in history someday.

One afternoon after John and I had returned back to Fort Sill after a mail run, we decided to get a shot of liquor before the big scheduled card game that night. As we approached the canteen, a white officer stopped us. He was an older Captain with an afternoon shadow on his face. He identified us, shook our hands. "It is a pleasure to meet you two fine gentlemen. My name is Captain Falkner. I have a bottle of whiskey, and I would be honored, if you would join me for a drink."

I answered "Sir with all due respect, the army doesn't allow white officers to drink with black enlisted members. Sir."

The Captain answered, "Any men that fought the Apache like the way I heard you fight can drink with me. And it don't matter what color you are." The Captain grabbed the fifth of whiskey and we grabbed our canteen cups and crouched around the bar. He filled both of our cups, and he drank the rest from the bottle. John and I watched the Captain drink, because we were flabbergasted with this situation.

"Well men, I guess you're wondering who the hell am I, and what am I looking for. Go ahead men drink up. Relax drink and I'll talk." He said. John and I began to sip. The captain continued, "Gentlemen, I'll give you the bottom line first. I'm recruiting two soldiers to join our unit. This unit is so special that I conduct my own recruiting quest. This unit is unique in its ability, and there is only one unit like this in the United States. I can't tell you what we do, but I can tell you what we don't do. We are under direct authority of the President. We don't guard trains, escort the mail, or conduct security patrols of those useless communication cables. We don't pull guard duty at the stockade. We don't pull KP or dig ditches. We don't for damn sure work for the wealthy. In this unit, if you make it through our tough training program, you will receive forty-five dollars a month, and live in a barracks, not a tent. In this unit you'll be treated as equals. My unit has a mixture of all types of people from around the world. I can tell you this if you make it through our rigorous training program, you'll be serving with the best of the best. Don't make a decision now. I'll be back tomorrow at the same time in a covered wagon. If you decide to go, get in the back, and you'll go back with me to your new home. If you decide not to join, it's ok, I'll understand." The Captain mounted his horse, looked at us and said, "I'll be back tomorrow."As he was leaving, he almost ran into Cactus. I was glad to see him. Cactus is a gold mine of information. Cactus knows everything that happens on this post.

I handed Cactus the cup of whiskey and asked, "Who's that guy, Cactus?"

Cactus replied, "He's called the shadow Captain. Little is known about him and his unit. He's as mystic as the shadow unit that he leads. What they do is some big secret." That next evening John and I decided to join. It wasn't a hard decision to make, especially after finding out that we had weekend KP duty. At exactly the specified time, the covered wagon appeared into town. We jumped in the back. The Captain was in the back. He quickly pulled the cover of the wagon down. He congratulated us and we were on our way. He pulled out a Bible and made us swear an oath of secrecy. At the end of the oath, he mentioned that if we were to break the oath, that we'd be imprisoned in the Federal pen. The Captain started to feed a little more information to us.

"Okay Men, here is a little more information about what we do. We don't fight Indians. We conduct missions after conventional and political means have been exhausted. The mission that we perform will never be published in the paper. Our table of organization is not set up like a normal conventional unit. You'll be placed in a team. Our jobs range from snipers, trackers, pioneers, signalmen, linguists, and many others. Currently we are undermanned by five slots. You'll be assigned a position after your profile has been evaluated. Your profiles are currently being assessed as we speak. By the time we make it to your new home, I should be able to assign you to your new job. Your training will start tomorrow." An hour later we made it to our destination. The Captain looked at us with a smile.

"Welcome, gentlemen, to your home. Come have dinner with me and I'll brief you on a few more details." John and I dismounted the wagon. I began to feel suspicious of the Captain's good manners and hospitality. After dismounting, we stood motionless, looking around at the immediate environment. The Captain's HQ building was a house. In fact all of the buildings were houses. There were no gates, guards, or even tents. I saw whites, blacks, Indians, and people of all types walking around in the area. I didn't see any uniforms except for those who had mixed uniforms with their civilian attire. There was nothing there that demonstrated to me that the area was a military establishment. John and I walked inside the Captain's Quarters, where the dinner table was already set for us. The Captain picked up where he left off.

"The missions that we conduct are tailor-fitted to the mission needs. Each one of those men that you saw out there is an expert at some trade. Sometimes you'll be required to act independently. In the type of missions that we conduct, capture is not an option. We are guerrilla fighters, and those are the tactics that we use. What we do is usually far beyond the call of duty. Here there's no recognition for valor. Success to us is mission accomplishment. Living or dying here is insignificant. The mission comes first, men come second. That is the main reason why accommodations here are so reasonable." He continued. "Our living conditions here are second to none. Most of the men that live in this compound have families. There's one more requirement that I have to tell you about before you make your final decision. If you decide to accept this unit, there will be little to no contact with the outside. You have sworn an oath to never, I repeat never talk about your mission to anyone." Suddenly, the Captain changed his focus. "You gentlemen smell that?" We all sniffed and could smell roast beef and garlic cooking. The Captain waved us on. "Lets go eat." Up to this point John and I hadn't sparked any conversation. The Captain had talked the entire time. We all stuffed ourselves with dinner like pigs.

"Sir, that's the best damn dinner that I've eaten since I've been in the Army. My compliments to your lovely wife sir," I told the Captain. The table was cleared and the Captain continued.

"Okay guys, where did I leave off? Oh yeah I remember," the Captain farted, "damn that was one hell of a dinner. Something else I'm sure that you noticed is that there are no minorities or majorities in this unit. I simply get the best. I don't give a damn what color people are. Discrimination in this unit will not be tolerated. The mission that we conduct calls for a focused individual that can put that type of bullshit aside." The Captain opened up and looked at two individual folders. "These folders contain your profiles. Okay men. Decision time. Do you accept to stay with us?"

I spoke for John, "Absolutely, yes," I answered, and John acknowledged by nodding his head.

The Captain continued, "John, you are a half-breed. Your mother is from the Shawnee tribe and your father fought and was killed in the civil war." Both John and I were surprised that the Captain had this type of information. John had never even told me that he was part Indian. "Your primary job with this unit is to become a unit tracker. Your alternate job will be a weapons specialist. Your training cycle will be a long one. It will last for at least three months. Unfortunately, gentlemen, after tonight you will not see each other for a long time. Mack, your primary job will be as a weapons specialist. I don't have much information on you Mack, but it is my gut feeling that you'll make a perfect weapons specialist."

The Captain personally escorted us around most of the day. This was his way of getting to know us. I was surprised to see that the unit was actually small in numbers. Military tradition and protocol was not a way of life. Most of the soldiers carried the weapon of their choice. Most of the soldiers were unshaven. There was no saluting. But the most unique fact about this unit was there was no unit designation. This inter-army society was so different and so unconventional that it made me wonder if it was actually legal to operate like this. Now I understood why Cactus didn't know much about this unit. This unit was the President's secret army. Two days later we reported to our training sites. I didn't see the Captain again for a long time. I was supposed to meet my new trainer at the mess facility that next morning for my first day of training. It was explained to me that this sergeant was supposed to be my mentor/counselor. He was assigned to me for the next three months. I figured that since the Captain was so mannerly towards me that maybe this sergeant would be the same. My spirit was high, and I was ready for training.

The door to the mess hall opened. My jaw dropped to the floor and my dream shattered to shit. It was Sergeant McCish.

The Irishman had that awful shit-eating grin on his face as he observed my look of astonishment. He instantaneously started on my nerves, "Well lad you want to be with the best, you want to be a weapons man?" I was too stupefied to answer.

I tried to stutter some words out, "Sergeant. I'm happy to see you."

The Sergeant grit his teeth, replied with a smile, "Somehow I don't believe that bullshit. You're not lying to me, are you Sergeant?" By now I figured that I had nothing to lose so I answered with my heart. I looked right in the eyes of that short arrogant bastard, and said, "Sergeant, there is nothing that you can do or say to shake my spirit. I've been through hell and back. So if you're going to holler at me, go ahead. If you're going to hit me, let's get it over right now. But if you're going to do neither here and now, do yourself and me a favor, and stay the fuck off my goddam back, please!"

McCish laughed, "Aw lad, that's the spirit that I was looking for. I knew you had it in you. It was the only way I knew to provoke a true response from you. With that said let's do some weapons training." McCish and I walked down to an old abandoned barnyard. We stopped at a covered wagon. McCish grabbed the covers on the wagon and stated, "Your training starts here lad." He unveiled the wagon's contents. The wagon was piled with all types of small arms weapons. McCish said, "For the next three weeks this is your place of duty. By the time that I finish with you, you must know how to assemble, dissemble, engage and acquire targets effectively. If by chance you screw this phase of your training up, you'll be booted back down to your old unit as a private. One week from today at sundown I will test you on each and every weapon. I will randomly pick at least ten weapons of my choice. To be on the safe side, learn them all. So pay close attention." One by one the sergeant explained each weapon with ease and confidence. My attention was focused because I had no intention to going back to that purgatory.

For the next three days, I lived at the range. I studied each and every functioning part of the weapons. I had spent numerous hours with Sergeant McCish during his after hours in going over nomenclature. I would then go into hibernation and assemble and disassemble the weapons. The old Irishman was just as committed in training me properly as I was to learning what he was teaching. It was a good mix for a healthy learning environment. However, I had no disillusion that McCish would not hesitate to flunk me if I screwed up the test. McCish was not a compassionate man. I also felt that it would be an insult to fail the people who invested the time and resources to train me, such as the Captain. But the main reason that I wanted to make it was because I owed it to myself. For once in my life I had control over my own destiny. Finally, the day of testing came. I was ready to get this phase behind me. The actual tester was a much younger Sergeant. McCish was there only as an observer. I guess this was their way of validating the test and removing any of the subjectivity. McCish gave me the thumbs up prior to the test. That made me feel good and confident

The tester stated rather coldly, "I will pick eight to ten weapons out of this wagon. You will not know which weapons that I'll pick because I'm gonna blindfold you. I will disassemble the weapons and mix up the parts. When I take off the blindfold you will have approximately one hour to reassemble, conduct a weapon check, state the nomenclature, and effectively engage targets based on the types of weapons capabilities. Do you understand what must be done?"

I nodded yes.

"Are there any questions," the proctor asked. I said no. He wished me good luck and put the blindfold over my eyes.

After the tester jockeyed around for twenty minutes, which felt like hours, he returned and took off the blind fold. "Remember you have one hour," the tester reminded me. I stepped back and took a deep breath. My strategy was to construct the rifles first because their parts were large and easy to identify. McCish was the time keeper. His job was to announce the time loudly on the minute. In less than one minute I had assembled my first weapon. I quickly started my presentation.

"This is a 44 Henry Lever Action Cartridge Magazine Rifle. It is shoulder fired, and fires 15 shots." I fired the weapon at the target located about 100 yards away. A distant but loud voice announced "55 minutes remaining." I quickly assembled the next weapon.

"This is the Winchester model 1873. It fires 12 shots. Its effective range isn't as great as the Henry, but its ammunition is universal with the Colt peacemaker handgun." I fired the target that was located at 75 yards as I explained. My confidence grew as I continued. I assembled the largest weapon on the table. "This is a heavy bore single-shot breech loaded weapon. This Sharps .50 caliber, or some call it the Big Fifty fires a 550-grain bullet with a 120-grain powder charge. Some use this weapon to hunt elephants. It has excellent range and superb accuracy if fired correctly." I fired at the target at 300 meters. In the background Sergeant McCish announced that there were 40 minutes remaining. I assembled the easiest weapon next. "This is the 10 gauge shot gun. Excellent for close in fighting." I blasted the 10 meters targets. "This is the 30-06 shotgun. It's good for opponents that like to hide behind walls and trees. In fact a direct hit from this weapon would split a man in half. In my opinion this is the best sniper rifle in the Army's arsenal." I shot at the target that was positioned 100 yards behind a tree. I assembled the smallest weapon on the table. "This little bugger is the 22 Derringer. It is a single shot weapon that uses percussion type ammo. Good as a last resort weapon and is effective up to 10-meter max." I stepped back from the table to collect my thoughts. There were at least three handguns left on the table. All the parts looked the same. "Thirty minutes," Sergeant McCish called out.The sweat on my brow began to bead. I lost 10 minutes piecing together a colt 45. The bodies of these weapons weren't difficult. The small intricate parts inside receiver were difficult to configure. The spring kept popping out.

"Finally, this is a 1873 Colt 45, which is a single action six shooter. It weighs two pounds and a couple of ounces. Its effective range is 100 yards," I said as I completed the task. "Twenty minutes and thirty seconds remaining." I had great difficulty in putting the next weapon together. "Seventeen minutes remaining," the Sergeant called out. After fifteen minutes I finally got the weapon assembled.

"This is the newer model of the 38 lightning or self-cocker. It has the same range as the Colt 45." I looked down and there was one more weapon that I had never seen before. "Thirty seconds remaining." I frantically tried to put the weapon together but it kept falling apart. "Time's up Sergeant Mack." My heart fell into my chest. Depression began to sink into my soul. The Sergeants were laughing. I couldn't understand why McCish came over to me and said, "Congratulations lad you passed the test 30 seconds ago. This weapon that you couldn't assemble was planted here to throw you off." I cried a sigh of relief.

"Good job lad. You broke the record in finishing this task. Don't get the big head because tomorrow morning you start phase two of your training, which will last five weeks. In this phase you must demonstrate that you've mastered those weapons. This phase is all practical application and is the most important part of your training."

Early that morning I reported to the abandoned shack that was located in the middle of a large open field. This secluded area was considered to be this unit's version of the firing range. I found it interesting how this unit cleverly camouflaged all their activity. McCish had already arrived at the range an hour before me. When I arrived McCish handed me two hip holsters. I looked at him with a puzzled look. He seemed to read my mind, because he answered my unasked questions.

"You must become proficient in the draw. I can't tell you about the missions that you will be conducting. Lad, you'll have to trust me, and I tell you now, that your natural reflexes will be the one element that will keep you alive in this business. Those issued Army holsters aren't worth the leather that they are made from. These civilian holsters will make it easier to get your weapon. The key to killing your enemy is accuracy. The idea is to spend less time bumbling around to get you weapon, and spend more time acquiring your target. This point of your training will be drawing the weapon correctly with your right hand. The next week we will concentrate on the left hand." Once again the old man was true to his word. Every day from dusk to dawn for the next two weeks, I practiced the draw. The old man watched my every move all day. He was relentless in coaching and critiquing my skills. Finally, I found the most comfortable drawing technique for me. It was unorthodox, but the cross-body technique worked best for me. The old man estimated my speed to be 1/10 to 1/20 of a second. At the end of the two weeks the old man was satisfied with my progress, but I had to ask him a burning question that I had thought about for about a week. "Sergeant McCish, why is it so important to draw both weapons instead of one?" I asked.

"Well lad, that's a simple question. Its very difficult to hit your target in a gunfight. However, you increase your chances on hitting something with two guns instead of one." He answered.

I was bewildered by his answer, "Sergeant that makes good sense, but I have to ask you, do these missions always end or begin with a gunfight?"

"No, in fact since I've been in this business, I have never been a gunfight. But in the event that it happens, you have to have an edge. Remember this young lad. The education that I'm giving you is only a drill, and that's all it is: a drill. It's easy to lose your nerve when facing down a man eye to eye. The ultimate purpose for this drill is to make you do what comes natural, without hesitation. It is the mere act of reacting instead of think-ing. I'm not saying that thinking isn't good, but there will be times that thinking isn't required, and when the time comes, you'll know."

The next two phases of training went by quickly. Phase three training lasted one week, and was spent conducting live firing for accuracy drills at the range. I worked on firing my 38 Lighting and Colt 45. Exercises like speed loading and rapid firing were rein-forced time after time. Phase four lasted another week, and com-bined phase two and three together. After four weeks of intense revolver training I felt confident, but in the back of my mind, a questioned still loomed. *Am I really ready to face another human being in a standup gunfight?* I felt that McCish had to be lying about not ever facing anyone in a standup gunfight. He knew too much. I guess killing another man in a gunfight isn't something to be proud of. Phase five was the last phase of my weapons train-ing. This phase lasted three weeks. The first week I qualified with all of my rifles.Over the next two weeks a team of professional unit snipers trained me. I learned the art of stealth. The grand finale was an exercise of stalking. This exercise lasted for three days. After three long months of extensive training, the end was here. The night before the graduation, Sergeant McCish and I talked about whatever came to mind.

"Well son, you've made it. You will never be the same for the rest of your life. From this point on you will bear the great respon-sibility of something that is much larger than life," McCish explained to me like a father who is having a heart to heart talk to his son.

"Sarg, with all due respect, since I've been here you've been talking in rhymes and riddles. This whole secrecy business has been one enigma after another. Since I've made it, could you please clue me the hell in," I asked with a bit of contempt in my voice. McCishes paused before responding and took a long drag off his wooden pipe.

With a slight grin, "In due time you'll understand the true meaning of responsibility. Now listen laddy, don't take it personal if I don't talk about the mission. As a matter of fact the mission isn't the issue, it's the responsibility here in this unit. Mission accomplishment in this unit is the number one goal in this unit, even if it requires giving up your life. You do it for God, and your country, you do it for the unit. You do it for me. I do it for you if necessary. We do this in exchange for the quality of life that we live at this compound. You will never see outside this compound a life like the one in which you will be living. I've lived in this secret society for at least 10 years. I left this unit time and time again, but I always come back. This time I'm here to stay, until I retire. I retire in three months. In fact, you are my replacement." Once again McCish caught me off balance. My suspicion about McCish came to an end. I admired his integrity, honor, and loyalty to the country, and the unit. This quality of commitment is what I wanted. I was touched, and I was sure that this unit was my true calling. It all made sense to me how and why McCish was so relentless during basic training and during my special unit training. McCish was secretly working during my basic training with the intention of conducting early recruiting. He followed the progress of the unit for months. Somehow, word got around of our progress. He found whatever characteristics he was looking for, in me. I gave the Sergeant a shameless grin.

"You know sergeant, I take back some of the bullshit that I said about you."

"Now, now, laddy don't get mushy on me," McCish said, smiling broadly.

I grinned and said, "Sarge I didn't say all of the bullshit." I graduated the next day, but there were no ceremony, no diploma, no band and no witnesses. There was only a handshake from Sergeant McCish.

CHAPTER 8
EVIL HOMBRES

Life at the compound was nice. If we weren't in a training cycle, off-hours activity meant fishing, hunting, whatever came to mind. I spent lots of hours having dinner with my peers' families. The only real limits that we had were that we were unauthorized to go outside of the compound. However, necessities that were needed were provided, free of charge. It was almost a paradise. This new-found freedom bothered me. I knew that there had must be a cost for all of these luxuries. After a month a euphoric lifestyle, the day of reckoning came. At 0300 Sunday morning the well-mannered Captain personally woke me up from a deep sleep. There was a small nudge on my shoulder and I heard him say the alerting code words, "Thunder Strike," which meant for me to be at the briefing within the half hour for the warning order. I dressed and made it to the Captain's house within 15 minutes.

The Captain was very informal with us at the briefing. It seemed to be more of a social gathering instead of military a briefing. There were only 8 of us at this briefing. The only ones that I recognized were McCish and the Captain. The Captain was standing in front of a map with a relaxed look on his face. In one hand he had a make-shift pointer and in the other hand he had a long brown-greenish stogy. The room was covered with maps, and on the tables there were pictures of individuals. I could tell that this would be a detail oriented briefing. The well-mannered Captain knew how to keep everyone's attention.

The smell of fresh coffee was brewing. The room was filled

with cigar smoke. And I heard him say, "Gentlemen, the wife is gonna cook breakfast for us this morning." The informalities came to a conclusion when McCish conducted a roll call. The room got quiet and the cigars and cigarettes were put out. The climate transformed into a conventional military style briefing. The well-mannered Captain started the greeting with, "Gentlemen, we are called once again to cut another cancerous tumor out of the side of our great government. I was personally briefed by the President of the United States behind closed doors. This mission is so secret that members of the Congress and the President's cabinet can't be trusted with this sensitive information. In the eyes of some government officials, this mission is considered illegal. We are the President's ace in the hole men. We have been asked to act immediately. The situation sounds simple, but the outcome potential is complex and could have an impact on the future relations with Mexico and other southern hemisphere countries. The simple situation is this, there are some powerfully bad people that shot up the Texas Border town of Brownsville one week ago. Political tensions are high between our two countries, because these bandedos escaped back across the border after they made a hit. Like a swarm of hungry locusts that steal all the nutrients from the land, the bandedo fed themselves by robbing and pillaging the boarding towns of its ammunition, weapons and money. These assets that they obtain feed the fuel of the fire, which enhance this misdirected movement. This movement has been festering like a sore. Tensions have always been high around that region and many wealthy Mexican land owners feel that they lost valuable territory to the United States when Texas seceded years ago. This feeling is deep and supported by many of the people and Mexican officials. To make matters worse, they outnumber the Texas rangers 4 to 1, and if the Army tries to capture the band and crosses the border, war would break out between the two countries. The Mexican Army is also caught in a dilemma.

If the Army openly opposes this group, the cause would grow throughout the region, because the leaders of this cause would automatically become maudlin. This cause has accumulated support in the past week. This growth has made its way on the bordering Indian Reservation territory. Word leaked out that once the Comencharos join this movement, that Fort Brown will be attacked. If this movement is successful, it will have enough weapons and arms to refit a small army. This event could potentially set off a number of reactions. The revolution will grow like wildfire. Within a year the current Mexican government could fold and war would break out between our two countries, and the reservations may align themselves with the Mexicans. It is totally an unstable situation. This situation has been closely monitored by one of our operatives for about a month. His team has been gathering information for about three weeks." At 0600 that morning the Captain had finished briefing the initial situational portion.

His beautiful wife broke up the briefing by telling the Captain that it was time for breakfast. The Captain jokingly said, "And now to real important issues. Lets go eat guys." We all ate like kings. I wondered if we were eating as if it were our last meal. I began to get suspicious of this operation of eight men against a movement of many. I thought "What in the hell can eight men do that two nations can't?" After breakfast and a couple of belches, we all went back down in the Captain's briefing room. Cigars and cigarettes were lit. Cups of coffee were consumed. Normal conversation filled the briefing room once again. After about a half-hour, the Captain made the transition back to the task at hand. "Before we get started, my wife will be serving fresh baked catfish and hushpuppies for lunch." The Captain cuts a long drawn out fart. "Damn that was a good breakfast." The room filled with laughter. The Captain began the formal briefing once again. "We know the situation. But you don't know the major players. I've obtained pictures of the people that are in charge of this movement. They are located on the table in front of you. The man responsible for the revolution is named retired General Cesar Carlos. Or should I say ex-General Carlos. He is well known in the Mexican military circles. Politically, he is the second strongest man in the Northern half of Mexico. He's got people believing that the land North of the Rio Grand belongs to Mexico. Mexican authorities are reluctant to move against him. His numbers of armed hooligans are staggering. It is believed that he has over 400 men in his organization. This man is too strong of a political figure for any man or country to handle currently. We're going after his Achilles heel: his lieutenants. Our targets will be Manual Rodreuiez, Samuel Cortez and Alex Ramos. Each of these men makes up Carlos' primary staff. These men hold the very fabric of the revolution together." The Captain passed around individual pictures of a man with a heavy beard. His face was blemished with holes. The only other distinct facial feature that I could pick up from the black and white photo were his ebony black eyes. The Captain continued, "This is Manual Rodreuiez 45 from Youcaton Mexico. He is the most ruthless of the bunch. He is Carlos' strong arm. However, ruthless as he may be, he's very clever and provides Carlos the control needed to command such an organization. He insures that strict discipline is maintained within the ranks. He's fanatical about military structure and the institution of sound tactics. He is also a West Point Graduate. He served as Carlos' assistant when they fought the French. This guy here is a real asshole."

The Captain passed around the pictures of the next man. There was nothing that is distinctive about this man's face, except that he was well shaven and wore a thick waxed handle bar mustache. The Captain continued, "This, my friends, is the brains of the movement. Samual Esteban Cortez, 47 from Mexico City. He's like the minister of propaganda, and heads the intelligence faction of the movement. He has numerous contacts in the US and Mexico. Carlos will not move without consulting Cortez first. Carlos won't shit unless Cortez checks his asshole." There was a moment of laughter. The Captain continued, "With the combination of Rodreuiez and Cortez, Carlos' reign of terror has been a success."

The Captain passes out his final picture. "Gentlemen, without this man the cause or revolution would whither away. Money and proper funding is the keystone for Carlos' Campaign. This man is Professor Alex Fernando Ramos, 54 from Bogata, South America. He provides the movement's means of funding. He's an expert at providing the public with misinformation. He is Carlos' campaign manager. He writes all of Carlos' speeches. He's opened many political doors for him. He is dangerous and highly educated." The Captain handed me a brown portfolio chalked with pictures and letters. He whispered to me, "This is a detailed analysis about this fellow. Study this man tonight at your leisure. Let me summarize what we are up against. Fort Brown is going to be attacked around the fourth of July, Independence Day. The Texas Rangers can't help and the Mexican authorities won't help. Our President doesn't want to risk war with Mexico. The ambassador of Mexico asked our President in confidence for assistance with this problem. Gentlemen, our mission is to disrupt Carlos' operation and to deny him further influence in of the Rio Grand Valley." The room filled once again with an uneasy quietness. The men shook their heads and mumbled, "I can't believe this bullshit." Eight men against many. The Captain allowed his audience to think, and allow the reality of the situation to soak. He walked behind a makeshift podium as if he were going to give a speech I was the rookie of the bunch and didn't know how to react. I had no reaction. The Captain responded with a cool composure, "Okay gentlemen. Relax, this is how I propose to do the job. It's really simple. Our operatives have been stalking Carlos for three straight weeks. They gathered information about

Carlos that demonstrates that he is a one-dimensional thinker. In other words, he's pretty stupid without his primary staff. We'll simply blind him, take away credibility, and stop his funding. Bottom line, we assassinate Cortez, Ramos, and if an opportunity allows, we'll hit Rodreuiez." The briefing lasted up to lunch. We would be leaving for our destination within the next two days. I stayed behind after the warning order was complete to go over a few more details with the Captain. We talked over the importance of my target. Eliminating Ramos was the key to the success of this mission. Failure or capture wasn't an option.

He congratulated me on being the best marksman in the unit. He also apologized to me about putting me in the mix at such an early stage. He said that he had to go with the best. I felt confident in my abilities, but the pressure began to mount as time went on. This mission was highly classified. If this mission were to fail most of the southern border states security would be compromised. History would have to be rewritten. Both countries wanted to eliminate the problem of Carlos, but neither country wanted to get their hands dirty.

Basically, our team broke up into pairs and traveled by different modes for security reasons. We were all to meet at a secret meeting point. This secret place was located five miles south of the town of Brownsville. We would link up with our operative at that point. His code-name was Cap. He was the operative that had been conducting surveillance on Carlos for the past month. Once we linked up with Cap, he would provide us with the latest and up to date information on Carlos.

Sergeant McCish and I traveled together, disguised as hobos. We were unshaven and wore ragged clothing. Our suitcases were burlap bags. Once we reached Laredo, we were supposed to clean up and buy horses to ride to Brownsville.

I had plenty of time to think when we were on the train. The main thought that came to mind was how we were supposed to conduct diplomacy through a gun-barrel. I opened up the port-folio that the Captain had given me at the briefing. This information covered everything known about my target as well as facts on the movement's origin. My target, Ramos was an interesting person. Ramos was an educated man that held many college degrees. He was a college professor by trade and taught graduate level political science and philosophy. He taught at the University of Bolivia. He was well respected and held a seat in Bolivian Parliament. He had tried to run for the highest political offices in the country. His enemies became many in his efforts to make it to the top and he was convicted of some type political scandal. He was ousted from his country.

A decade later, he once again appeared in the Mexican political arena. He was responsible for assisting the current political government to victory over the old regime. The current regime became uncomfortable with Ramos' political goals, and he later became a serious threat. He was detained by the Mexican secret service and thrown in prison. Carlos and Ramos became close associates while serving time together. Carlos had been convicted of treason against the government and was serving a life term. Rodreuiez was Carlos' second in command while Carlos was jailed. Rodreuiez caught word that he was the next victim targeted for treason violations. Rodreuiez responded by leading 100 dedicated followers to pull a reprehensible ploy. Cortez, another one of Carlos' primary staff officers, masterminded a plan to break Carlos out of prison. Cortez lead an assault on the Commanding General quarters, killing the general's personal guards, servants, family and the Commanding General. None were spared.

The prison that housed Carlos was located five miles down the road. The bulk of the prison guards were compelled to respond to the hostile gunfire at the Commanding General quarters. The defense posture of the prison lowered when the majority of the guards left to assist the Commanding General.

Cortez deception plan worked. Rodreuiez assaulted the prison and overpowered the remaining few guards that were left behind. Carlos was set free. Carlos knew that Ramos' term in prison was almost over. Months later Carlos funded the best lawyers in the country to get charges against Ramos dropped. One week later after Carlos escaped, charges against Ramos were dropped. Sergeant McCish and I sat in opposite corners of the wooden boxcar discussing my target. He too was given the same portfolio on Ramos. He was assigned to conduct the hit, but my marksmanship scores were much higher than his were. I looked at the Sergeant. I could tell that he was uncomfortable in the boxcar. The high temperature in the boxcar made it like an oven. I figured I'd take a break and spark a response from the old warrior.

"Sergeant McCish I thought you told me that you'll be retiring within the next months." I asked.

"Yes, laddy, this is the last one for me," McCish responded.

"I've got to know, Sergeant McCish, how many missions will this be for you?" I asked. McCish started to count on his fingers and then pulled off his boots to count to count his toes. I looked at the Sergeant like he'd lost it. He looked at me and said sarcastically, "Can I borrow your fingers and toes? Damnit, I've seem to lost count. Can you help me man?" I was amused by his humor, and we both chuckled at his answer. It was his way of telling me that it was none of my business. I finally got the message not to discuss the past with the Sergeant.

"You win. But why did you volunteer for this mission?" I wanted to know. McCish looked me straight in the eyes, and said, "I didn't volunteer. Lad, if you miss or something or an unforeseen event comes up I'm your backup. Make no mistake about it. Ramos dies or we all die. Failure is not an option." McCish eventually fell into a deep sleep and I continued to study my portfolio notes. Ramos seemed to be the only legal key to Carlos' cause. This bothered me because Ramos was the only legitimate citizen that had done no wrong. And yet he'd been targeted as the primary hit. This provoked my thought process. I wondered if McCish were there to insure that the job was done if I hesitated.

Ramos was a smart public relations man for Carlos. His campaign tools included food for the starving, shelter for the homeless, and empty promises of liberty for the ones who listened to his message. Carlos' movement grew with every passing moment. Ramos was the pied piper and gathering more rats every day for the cause. The wealthy were afraid of Carlos because he could potentially bankrupt the landowners by ruthlessly destroying farms and crops. He'd been known to set fire to fields of sugarcane and coffee and bring businesses to their knees. Carlos ruled by intimidation. Anyone that opposed him pays the costly price of death.

There was nothing more in the portfolio to read. It was hard for me to believe that a man like Ramos was targeted for assassination. However, it made sense to me that I was given this target, because Ramos was the least guarded. I was impressed with the volume of information that was provided by the Mexican authorities. I guessed Carlos was more of a threat to them than he was to us. In any case, I felt that the mission was chalked with danger. I was sure that the event would be the most difficult thing that I'd ever faced.

A couple days later, the train stopped in Laredo. We replenished ourselves with food and water. However, McCish and I decided to continue our train ride further south to the town of McAllen, which was about another full day train ride. McAllen would put us even closer to the town of Brownsville. About mid-afternoon somewhere between Laredo and McAllen, the train came to a sudden halt, tossing us both into the hard wooden walls of the boxcar. We were both stunned by our collision with the walls. Dust and dirt clouded our view of what had happened. We could hear passengers screaming and panicking from the passenger cars. I saw McCish peaking through a small crack in our boxcar. I continued to scramble to find my weapons, which had been tossed somewhere up under the hay within the boxcar. McCish looked at me, *"Shhh...Listen."* The only thing that I heard was the puffing of the steam from the train's engine and the screaming of women. Suddenly, I heard gunfire. I quickly moved toward another peep-hole to see what was going on. The train was being robbed. I immediately thought, "Carlos." We didn't have to find him. He found us. Was it fate or was it luck. I was paralyzed with surprise.

Their guns fired at the train cars, splintering wood-chips and glass in every direction. We hugged the floor, trying to stay out of the way of bullets. They were firing directly into the flanks of the passenger cars. They showed no compassion for the men, women, or children. After a few minutes of intense gunfire, the carnage ended. Carlos' gangs of thugs were in control of the train and entered the train. My heart was pumping uncontrollably. I felt defenseless because my weapons were lost somewhere, tucked up under the hay. If we moved, we'd be heard. There was nowhere to run. We were trapped. Three men approached our car. The door began to open. Suddenly gunfire erupted in the vicinity of the passenger car. The three thugs left quickly to respond in the direction of the turbulence. The door remained half opened, so we could plainly see what was going on. There were at least 20 men lined up in a straight line. It looked like they were lined up for an interrogation. The thugs went through the line beating the defenseless passengers to the ground. I looked behind me and saw that my weapons were just an arm's length away, tucked under a bail of hay. Just as I was reaching for my weapons, I heard the word "Fire."I look in pure shock as my body stiffened with apprehension, and I watched a maniacal act unfold before my eyes. The bodies of 20 men fall to the ground as Carlos' men gunned them down. I could hear the screaming of women and saw the stream of blood flow from the direction of the innocent victims. I could do nothing but listen and look. I could feel anger and pain run within me. I had no idea that this level of barbarity could be achieved. I stared at the dead, and wanted to throw up, but the anger held the vomit back. These villainous acts continued, and again the thugs gathered the remainder of the women and children out of the train. People were dragged and beaten into a mass formation once again. This time the thugs tried to quiet the crying and screaming women down. This time a large heavyset bandito appeared in front of the group. He stood at least 6ft 2in and was elegantly dressed in dark clothing. The black sombrero, pearl handled pistols, and the black laced pants identified this man as Carlos. He calmly asked something about some Yankees that had boarded the train. I quickly assumed that a leak compromised our mission. He paced back and forth in front of the panic stricken crowd. Within minutes, he stormed away. The massacre ended as quickly as it started. The gang of thugs stormed away hurriedly with their guns blazing. This tragic event totally changed my attitude on the mission and my outlook on life. Before the atrocious event happened, I had mixed feeling about killing a man like Ramos, but then I was totally committed to ensuring that the innocent would be redeemed for this day of infamy. I was touched, and then the secret war had become personal. It became an eye for an eye mission. I had an empty void in my soul, and the only way to fill that void was to seek revenge. *Kill by gunfire, kill with a ruthless attitude and be unmerciful to the thugs that committed this manslaughter,* I told myself. I felt that I had been raped of my innocence and compassion. I was now becoming an empty shell. I had morphed into something that I'd thought I'd never become: a killer. I couldn't wait for the day to come when I would meet Senor Carlos and his band of thugs on a level playing field.

June 30, 1876

We linked up with the operative and the team three days later. Sergeant McCish told the Captain what had transpired on our trip. The Captain said that the mission wouldn't be aborted because nobody knew how much information had been leaked out. The cabin was located just five miles south of Brownsville. It was a hot and humid night, and the moon was full. The mosquitoes were as large as horse flies. All eight of us cramped into the log cabin for the meeting, which was standing room only.

The operative and the Captain had posted maps along the wall. Once again I could smell the strong odor of coffee brewing. The door opened. The Captain and two others walked into the crowded room. This time the mood wasn't as festive as the first briefing. The focus was to get the job done. The Captain immediately started the briefing at 930 p.m. "Gentlemen, I want to introduce you to our operative: Major Marcos," Marcos had a shadowy look. He was tall and wore dark clothing. He was well armed with pistols: two hip holster pistols and two shoulder holsters pistols. He was covered with trail-dust. The Captain began, "Before the Major gets started I have a few more things to share with you. First the Major used to be my boss, so be on your best behavior. Second, I'm compelled to move the timetable up because of some new developments. The Carlos movement has gained a significant amount of momentum in the Mexican congress. It is believed that a coup will take place sometimes after the fourth of July. Bottom line, it is highly imperative that we disrupt Carlos' operation before matters get worse." The Captain finished his speech and moved to the rear of the room.

The operative stood up and began to make his way to the front, as all eight set of eyes watched his movement. He began talking as he was moving, "My name is Major Dubois Marcos. I at one time served in your unit. I work for your counter intelligence group. I've been operating in this region for approximately two and a half years. I've been monitoring Carlos for a couple of months. The Captain was right about the timetable. Our orders are to initiate this mission immediately. Carlos and his 200-man army are currently located in the town Larcosis, Mexico. They will operate from there up to the evening of the 3rd of July. They have just finished successfully conducting a month long reign of terror and destruction along the Southern border of the Rio Grande. Sergeant McCish and Sergeant Mack personally attest to how they operate. They witnessed their methods of brutal intimidation and humiliation. They have been successful in their movement along the border because they are being aided by the Comencharos as guides along the vast area of the Rio Grande. They use the town of Larcosis for a safe-haven. The people of this town are sympathetic towards Carlos' cause. Ramos will link up with Cortez in Monterey on the third of July with treasury notes. Only Carlos, Cortez, and Ramos know of the money. The money will be used to purchase ammunition for the shipment of guns that will also arrive with Ramos. These Spensor Henry rifles are part of a deal between the Comencharos and Carlos. If the weapons make it to the Comencharos, they will become allies with Carlos and attack Camp Brownsville. The Captain and I have more planning to do, so get some rest and we'll get started tomorrow on how we plan to conduct this job."

EARLY MORNING 1ST JULY 1876

It was early morning of the first of July. The night before, Carlos and Cortez had been celebrating their spoils of victory at the local canteen.

Cortez was well respected by the locals, and at one time lived in the vicinity. In his early youth he lived in a poverty-stricken area outside the city. His high IQ, and the local Catholic priest got him an education. He had a successful military career of fighting the French. Cortez became Carlos' confidant in the early years and has remained that way for years. He had always been envious of the American lifestyle. He always felt that the Americans had always looked down on the way Mexicans live. He was a fanatical about patriotism, loyalty to God and his country. His methods of intelligence gathering were second to none. His connections with the underworld in Mexico and America made him an even more valuable asset to Carlos. This was how the leak may have occurred. After a party the night of June 30, Cortez was having a drink with a local bar girl. Francisca was a beautiful long haired brunette that enjoyed the nightlife. Nobody in the town except for one person knew that Francisca was a double agent. Prior to meeting Cortez, she sold her services to Major Marcos.

She told Marcos about the shipment of weapons. Marcos' other operative that worked for him had been stalking Ramos. Marcos pieced together that Ramos was in charge of delivering the guns and money. Cortez, who had known Francisca for years before Marcos knew her, approached her with double the amount of money that Marcos had paid. Cortez was the only other person that knew that Francisca was a double agent, and could be bought out. She told Cortez what she knew about information that she sold to Marcos. She gave Cortez a tip that the weapons would be intercepted in Monterey on the third of July. What she didn't know was that Marcos also knew that Francisca was a double agent. He sold her misinformation to be used for deception measures as added cover for the primary target. She had deducted that the primary target wasn't the weapons, but she would not be able to warn Cortez because he had already left town to act on this misinformation on the early morning of the first of July.

Early morning second of July at 0200, I was awaked by the Operative. "Be prepared to move in five minutes." I hurriedly gathered my belongings. My saddle bags had already been prepared and weapons were assembled the night before. There was no time for any planning. I met Marcos and three of my peers as they were mounting their horses. I noticed that McCish wasn't with them. I figured he knew my heart, and he knew that I meant business. As I was mounting my horse, Marcos quickly gave us a situation update, "Sorry about the uncomfortable night but we have to move now. Cortez moved out late last night with about fifty banditos. We need to get there before he employs his security. The mission stays the same." I was tired but the ride to Monterey was fast and hard. The early morning breeze woke me. It was an all-day ride and we took only a few breaks. Finally we reached the outskirts of town at dusk. We stopped momentarily to link up with two more operatives. Apparently Marcos had already anticipated this move. The guides were there to move everyone into position. This ploy was to save time. Marcos issued his last orders, "Before everyone disappears, remember that it is highly important to be in position within the next hour. Don't forget we don't go back until Ramos is dead or we are dead. Ok men good luck." Marcos and I slithered our way through the maze of alleys to ensure that we wouldn't be detected. The alleys were empty, but the streets were full of activity. I could hear the nightlife activity of pianos, jubilant laughter, and scattered fireworks. Something festive was going on. Fifteen minutes later, we stopped at a very large chapel that overlooked the town. I assumed that was our destination. The operative knocked at the door, and it opened within seconds. A beautiful brunette answered the door. We quickly jumped inside, and she frantically closed the door. Another one of Marcos' operatives was there. The operative updated Marcos with the latest information, "Cortez made it in town two hours ago. He has not deployed his guards yet. They are all drunk for now."

"Have the explosives been set and ready to go?" Marcos asked the operative.

"Si," replied the operative. He continued, "I must go now, I'll meet you on the other side of the bridge." He left to move into position. The lady and I stared at each other the whole time that Marcos was talking to his operative. I was uncomfortable with her feminine presence. I'm sure that she was uncomfortable with me because I was black.

Marcos looked at the both of us and said, "Relax, she's with us. I want you to meet Francisca."

In a polite voice she said, "please to meet you." "Likewise mam." I replied. That was a lie. I felt uncomfortable with her presence, not only because she was a woman, but because I had a gut feeling that she couldn't be trusted. We made our way up to the loft. Finally, we made it to the floor up under the bell tower. I said to Marcos while breathing heavily, "Shit Sir. The damn clouds might get in the way of my sight." Marcos looked at me and laughed. I immediately began to assemble my 30.06 and sharp 50 caliber rifles. We moved up to the windows to look for the best vantage points. Marcos pointed out the direction of where the targets would be located. Francisca interrupted Marcos and I. "Cortez has too many guards. What can we do to prevent the weapons from being unloaded off the train?"

Marcos replied, "We're not going for the weapons. We're going for a human target." Francisca looked puzzled and moved back into a dark corner of the room.

I explained to Marcos, "All I need is one shot. One shot one kill."

Marcos replied, "You'll actually need two, or perhaps three."

Francisca started to ponder once again, "What does this have to do with the shipment of weapons? Oh I get it, you're setting up some type of diversion that will allow you to get to the weapons." Marcos and I both stared at her for a moment.

Marcos answered, "Yes honey, you're a smart woman how did you know?" Marcos asked her, "Francisca could you go untie the bell tower rope. We'll need that rope for our escape." Marcos cleverly led her out of the room so he could continue discussing his plan with me. "This is a simple plan. The train will stop next to the coal shaft in order to reload. Cortez is to greet Ramos in order to give him the money to buy ammunition for all of those weapons that are loaded on the train. Ramos has to dismount the train by walking on the ramp to meet Cortez. Remember when I said you may possibly need three shots. The first shot is for Ramos. The second shot is for the explosives to detonate, to destroy the weapons, and the third is for Cortez if time allows."

"What the hell am I shooting at to cause a detonation?" I asked with concern.

Marcos answered, "All you have to do is aim at the top barrel. It is loaded with nitro. It's been padded, so the only thing that is missing is a bullet. Just hit Ramos, the barrel, then Cortez." Marcos made it sound easy. Marcos concluded with, "When it's all over, I've positioned our guys to cover us along the escape route. The risky part of the plan is our escape out of this position." I felt confident that the plan would work. It seemed that Marcos had worked out the plan down to the smallest detail, except for our escape out of the chapel. It was difficult to see everything clearly because it was dark. We both decided to take turns watching. I took the first watch. We would look once again in the morning at the first sight of daylight. Francisca slept on the floor near the door. It was 11:30 pm on the second of July. The train would arrive at 0800 the next morning.

0630 3rd of July, 30 Minutes before the Train Arrival

Time was creeping by at a snail's pace. Activity in the streets increased with the passing moment. The morning sun was beaming down. Incandescent light bounced off the buildings and left no shadows. The downtown circle that was full of life the night before took on an arid look in the morning. The confetti and bottles littered the streets. People began to trickle in from somewhere. I'd been awake since 0600, continuously playing the situation in my head. I kept asking myself why and how it would work? I kept drawing a blank. I wondered, was this plan of God's will, or was I there to carry out this deed for the devil? I had hoped that I was picked as an angel of vengeance to strike down this movement that started in Hell. Was this situation part of the devil's sick sense of humor, waiting for the final punch line? The only rational reason that I could come up with was that this was a sign of the times. It was a time when guns were the answer. Whether one was on the side of the good or bad, black, white, rich, or poverty-stricken, it was insignificant. In any case I had to quit thinking, because my thoughts kept running in an endless circle.

Activity in the streets increased. Train station offices were beginning to open. Carlos' men began to appear like roaches coming out of the woodwork. Some were bearded and unshaven, some had pot bellies, and some were slender in build. All had one thing in common: they were all heavily armed. I heard a disturbance that was moving in the direction of the train station. I didn't want to move because I wanted to stay focused on my target area. Marcos and Francisca scrambled towards the side window to see what caused the disturbance. I looked over in Marcos' direction and heard him say, "Shit." Francisca recoiled in horror. 0650 the disturbance in the street got louder and was making its way near my targeted area. Banditos left my targeted area to join in on this activity. I was able to track this activity with my scope as the mass of banditos moved towards my targeted area. When I saw what the activity was about, I stared in horror. One of the operatives had been captured. He was being tortured and humiliated in the streets. He was kicked around like an animal. Blood was running out of every orifice of his body. His trail of blood ran down the dry dusty street. I thought to myself, "What a sick fuckin form of entertainment." Then I remembered some of the faces of the innocent victims that I witnessed Carlos' men slaughter. The fire in my gut rekindled once again. I wondered if there was another leak. Marcos must have been thinking the same thing. I looked at Marcos. Marcos looked at Francisca, and Francisca's eyes widened incredulously. Suddenly, events took off faster than I could comprehend. I could hear but not see the distant train blowing its horn. Cortez appeared out of the crowd to administer more pain to the captured operative. I looked back at Marcos, wondering if this mission was going to be aborted. Marcos stood up and started approaching Francisca, pulling out his knife. I quickly refocused on my targeted area. The crowds of banditos were in the center sector of my targeted area. The tension in my gut began to twist as the train approached out of the horizon. I listened to Marcos' angry form of interrogation of Francisca.

"You bitch. What did you tell them?" Marcos asked the petrified double agent. I could hear her back up towards the corner of the room.

She replied sheepishly. "Tell whom, what?" Marcos lunged at her, pinned her against the wall, grabbed her by her skinny neck, and with his other hand put the dagger to her throat. Marcos' angry tone was low, and his action about finding out what was going on was absolute. He continued to cross-examine her by starting with a threat, "If you give away this position I'll get it over with now and cut your damn throat. No more games, bitch." I looked back at Marcos' unyielding method to get the truth, as he slightly twisted the dagger in Francisca's throat and pierced the skin, causing blood to drain down her body. She stared at Marcos in fascinated horror. My face contorted with agony as I watched Francisca. I had to refocus on my target area as the train was now coming to a grinding halt. The sweat on my brow began to accumulate into small beads. I heard Francisca faintly cry out, "Okay Cortez knows."

"Cortez knows what?" Marcos asked angrily.

My finger was now glued to the trigger and my eyes were focused like an eagle honed in on its prey. With my other eye I could see Cortez kicking the captured operative in the street. He then pulled out his pistol and blasted the operative in the head. Then I heard Francisca cry out,

"He knows about you intercepting the weapons. I swear to you he knows nothing else." I then heard her body drop to the ground. I looked back and saw her body lying in a puddle of blood. I quickly refocused on my target. I assumed that the mission hadn't been totally compromised, and it was still a go. I wanted to focus my sights back on the targeted area, but I was burdened with compassion for Francisca's untimely death. I thought about the barbaric act that Marcos just committed. I hadn't fired a shot and already two were dead. Marcos moved over to my position. The train stopped. Marcos started to whisper in my ear.

"The mission has changed. Your targets are Cortez, Ramos, and then the weapons." I looked at Marcos with disbelief. Marcos began to explain, "Look there's not a lot of time, but now you need to know the real truth. I work directly for the President of the United States. I'm an officer of the secret service counter intelligence division. I've been chasing Cortez for two years. My mission is to eliminate Cortez and his spies. He has been the main organizer for terrorists against the U.S. for years. This mission was so secret that your Captain didn't even know. I had to use you guys in order to get to Cortez. Carlos is just a figurehead. Cortez is the real power of the movement. You'll have to trust me. I know your commitment to the unit. But if we miss getting Cortez, many more innocent victims will die. If you get Ramos, and only Ramos, some other asshole will replace him. Cortez cannot be replaced." The door to the train opened and people began to trickle out. Marcos got closer to my ear as I was narrowing in on the exit door of the train.

"Damnit, listen to me Mack. Francisca was a double agent. I purposely fed Francisca this information knowing that she would sell this information to Cortez. This leak caused Cortez to expose himself here. It was the only way that I could isolate Cortez. If we're gonna die today, make it count for something." My trigger finger began to sweat. Cortez approached the train exit door, hand stretched out ready to welcome Ramos. I felt that I had reached an untraveled territory in my life. I entered this mission with a set of rules, and now that game was ready to conclude, and all of the rules had changed. Ramos walked out and Cortez immediately grabbed and embraced him in his arms. I had to make the choice. My front sight post of my weapon swung towards Ramos, and then swaggered in the direction of Cortez. Both of the Bandito leaders approached the off ramp of the train. As the two leaders walked off the ramp, Ramos reached in his overcoat pocket and pulled out what I believed to be the bank draft. Marcos made a last desperate effort to sway my decision process.

"Dammit Mack, Cortez is the reason why we're both here. Shoot that son of a bitch first. Do your country a favor and rid the earth of this scum!"As Cortez grabbed the alleged bond, I squeezed the trigger. The round hit Cortez, entered through his forehead, and exited through his temple, throwing brainmatter, flesh, and blood all over Ramos. This event happened so fast that Ramos still had the document in hand, and watched Cortez's body fall to the ground. Time seemed to stop for a second. The activity in the street stopped, and Carlos' men were paralyzed with confusion. With no leadership directing traffic, thirty to forty men in the street frantically pulled out their pistols. Like a bunch of disorganized ants, the masses scurried around, bumping into each other, trying to figure out who did what. I quickly jumped back up into my sniper position to find my next target. I saw that Ramos had quickly ducked behind a large wooden cargo container. I immediately dropped my 30.06 rifle and picked up my sharps buffalo rifle. My sights were set on the corner of the wooden cargo box where I thought Ramos was hiding. I fired my simi cannon. The round went straight through the wooden container, sending wood-chips in every direction. By the time I chaotically re-bolted another round in the chamber, Ramos panicked at this unnerving sight, and tried to bolt back to the exit doors of the train. The micro-second before he successfully made it to the door, I squeezed another round off and caught him in the upper part of his torso. The slug ripped his arm completely off except for a thread of flesh that barely held. The impact of the round sent him crashing into railings of the train. All the banditos couched behind some sort of cover, and watched in stunned silenced Ramos' blood-spewing contorted body. By the time I re-bolted another round into the chamber, the rain of lead hit our side of the building. That third shot gave away our position. There was nothing that we could do but hug the ground. Bullets were zinging in every direction. There was no way that I could go for the third target without getting hit. Wood chips, glass and dust restricted my vision. For the moment, all we could do was to cover our heads. For the moment we were helpless. We needed a diversion now. Our only hope was to make it through the escape hatch. But the bullets kept piercing through the wood. The wooden church offered little to no shielding. Was this an omen? I couldn't move an inch without feeling the heat of the bullets sizzling around me. I knew I'd get hit by hot lead in matter of seconds. In a moment of desperation, Marcos jumped up with his Henry rifle and fired at the barrel that was laced with nitro. He missed and in his effort, was struck by a bullet, knocking him back against the wall. He fell to the floor and rolled toward the escape hatch, leaving a trail of blood from his wound. As fortune would have it, the banditos focused their fire in the direction to the area where Marcos fired. This caused the diversion that I needed. I picked up my sharps rifle and fired. Kaboom! A colossal ball of fire, smoke and debris flared up the area, sending Carlos' men hurling through the air. The ones that were closer to the train ran through the streets and lit up like human torches, crying in shrills of pain and agony. Suddenly the train car carrying the weapons and gunpowder imploded, which sent another shock wave of fire, dust, and smoke through the air, mangling anyone in its destructive path. By the time the smoke cleared, Marcos and I made our way through the trap door of the bell tower. Carlos' men must had been momentarily stunned by the explosions, because the gunfire ended. The escape plan was also designed to be simple. The escape hatch lead to a ladder that lead to the outside rear of the church. We were supposed to use the buildings located in the alley to cover our movement. Our snipers were strategically positioned to cover our move through the town.

One mile east of town was a bridge that divided the town from the poverty stricken suburbs. There were sympathizers for our cause there that were suppose to aid in our escape.

The bridge was being rigged with explosives. In summary, the plan was to fight our way to the far side of the bridge. We were supposed to consolidate on the far side, and then blow the bridge. Afterwards the local sympathizers were to aid our escape. As I landed on the ground in the rear of the church, I heard the front door of the church being kicked in. We both heard the pattering of feet run up the stairs, to the loft of the bell tower. At a quick pace we moved through the maze of buildings in the alley. We hugged the side of the buildings hoping that they would offer some concealment. We didn't have cover from the first one of our snipers because he was the operative that was captured. Thus we had to hurry and try to make it to our second position for sniper coverage. We couldn't move too fast because Marcos' wound slowed his movement. So far our movement had been unopposed but our luck was about to change. As Marcos and I were moving in haste down the alley, an inconceivable situation developed. Five of Carlos' men hurdled themselves from between two building into the alley, and we all collided with each other. We were all thunderstruck about how close we were to each other.

My rifle had been knocked out of my hand. Marcos' shoulder was dripping blood. These Banditos weren't about to leave empty handed. Who would take the lead? Who was going to initiate the gunfight? I was sure that Marcos was thinking the same thing as I. Capture isn't an option. It was going to be my first true test of a face to face gunfight. Time seemed to stop until this matter was settled. We were at least an arm's distance away from each other. We stared at each other, looking, waiting, and waiting. All that we needed was a twitch or a blink of an eye. I glanced at Marcos. He had angry eyes, and he stood still like a statue.

I figured that he had isolated the two or three banditos that were closer to him. This left me with the two that were closer to me. I looked in their eyes. The one that was the furthest away had eyes that were sunk in the back of his skull. He was scared. The one to my front right flank, looked at me, and his eyes widened with alarm. Finally a secondary explosion was heard from a distance. Both Marcos and I drew our weapons at the same time, but unfortunately, Carlos' men did the same. There was a convergence of gunfire from both sides. My training had taught me to draw both six-shooters and fire with accuracy. The two that were closer to me fell to the ground as the bullet holes left smoke and blood pulsating from their chests. Marcos was only able to draw one six-shooter, but with machine gun reflexes he was able to get the two that were closer to him before the third one was able to get off a second round that hit Marcos in the same wounded shoulder. The impact of the round knocked Marcos to the ground. Immediately Carlos' man bolted in the opposite direction and tried to evade death. It was too late. I capped three rounds in his back. At once, I reloaded as I went to aid Marcos, who was lying in his own puddle of blood.

Marcos' skin was clammy, and he was gritting his teeth from the pain of his wounds. I looked at his wounds. One bullet wound had entered his left arm. The nastier bullet wound entered his left shoulder. There was no time to dress the wounds because I knew the others had heard our gunfire. I grabbed him by his other arm and tried to pick him up. Marcos let out a cry of pain. "Oh shit, Mack don't move me. Don't. For the love of God, don't. I'm all used up." In a faint tone Marcos said, "Kill me, save yourself, kill me, kill." Marcos blacked out. All we had to do is to make it to the next position, which was about another 200 yards. Our covering fire was suppose to be located there. I had to make a quick decision to either leave Marcos and save myself or try to carry Marcos, or stay and fight until help would arrive. Well, I knew that I could leave Marcos to be captured alive, and staying to fight was out of the question. It became a moot point, because the bullets started zinging in every direction. Carlos' men were once again on our trail. I immediately draped Marcos over my shoulder and sprinted towards the next position. As I was running, I could see bullets bouncing against the buildings and the kicking up of dust. I glanced back and about 20 of Carlos' men were chasing me. I just kept running. I felt a bullet tear into my side. It burned, but I kept moving. I could feel my blood running down my leg. My shoulders were beginning to cramp. The heat, humidity, sweat and Marcos' blood dripping body loosened my grip. I was getting exhausted and my legs began to cramp. I no longer had control over the situation. There was time for a reaction, because I could no longer go another step. I ran into the closest building that offered me some form of cover. It was a horse corral. I threw Marcos' limp body to the ground and loaded my sharps buffalo rifle. Carlos' men were about 100 meters away and running idiotically out in the open. I tucked myself between a bail of hay and under a wooden corral door gate. Carlos' men had closed at 75 yards. I took aim at the first bandito that entered my scope: head shot. The impact of the bullet exploded his head into pieces. I bolted another round into the chamber: chest shot. The impact of the round bolted the bandito through the air, and onto his back. I bolted another round into the chamber, but this time the banditos closed their distance to 50 yards.

The bullets were now focused in my vicinity. Woodchips, hay and dust impaired my vision. This time I knew deep in my heart that I would run no more. If the angels of death were singing I wasn't listening.

By now Carlos' men were firing and moving, using anything to shield their advance. One bandito hid behind a wooden water trough. The other hid behind a horse. I fired a round that penetrated the wooden trough, and the impact of the bullet hit the bandito directly in the face, and split his head in half. I bolted another round into the chamber and fired at the horse. The horse panicked and knocked the bandito into a hail of bullets that were meant for me. I reached into my pocket and felt around my ammunition belt some more ammo, but there was none. It didn't matter because now the banditos were almost at rock throwing distance. I was getting desperate because the only ammunition that I had remaining was the ammunition that was left in the chambers of my six-shooters. I wanted to grab Marcos' weapons but it was too late. I jumped up and moved into the shadowy rear of the corral. Carlos' men began to pour through the corral gates. There were more of them than I had bullets.

An angel of mercy must had been on my side. Carlos' men were beginning to fall down. *Thank god for my covering fire,* I thought. After three to four of the banditos fell dead from the plunging fire of our snipers, Carlos' men withdrew from their attack. I crawled over to Marcos. He was still alive but was out like a light. I bandaged up Marcos' wounds, just enough to stop the bleeding. I tied my shirt tight around my waist to stop me from bleeding. Once again I draped Marcos over my shoulder and walked for another 200 yards to an abandoned barn located on the near side of the bridge. I met one of our team members, who was a sight for sore eyes. Our instructions were to wait until one of Marcos' operatives made contact with the sympathizers that opposed Carlos' movement.

After thirty minutes of waiting, the heat in the barn became unbearable. The shirt that I had used for a makeshift bandage started to cut into my side, and the pain was agonizing.

Without warning, the bridge that was the gateway to our freedom exploded into tiny pieces. Gunfire erupted and ended on the far side of the bridge. We were in total awe. The only thing that we could figure out was that Carlos' men must have sprung a trap. The operative must have blown the bridge to warn us. Now we ran into a different set of problems. We were cut off from our escape route. Carlos' men were still in town, and probably trying to figure out how they were going to attack us. We were low on ammo, food and water. If Marcos and I didn't get to a doctor in the near future, we were dead. We stayed in the barn. If they attacked, this would be our last stand.

Later on that evening, I noticed a man on top of a float drifting across the lake to our side. It was one of Marcos' operatives. My team member fished him from the lake and brought him to our position. His body was riddled with bullets and bleeding profusely. He told us that Carlos' men had already been waiting on the far side of the bridge, to cut off any chance of escape. After the firing died down in town, Carlos' men saw the operatives thinking that they were us. The ambush was triggered, and the operative that was setting the charge was hit by a bullet. He inadvertently fell on top of the plunger and blew the bridge by accident. We assumed the reason that Carlos' men discontinued their pursuit is because Carlos' men thought that we were all dead. Moments later Marcos' man died.

The air in the barn was stale. The heat from the beaming sun turned the barn into an oven. The sun beat through the cracks of the barn and caused a glare. Marcos began to moan from the pain of his wounds. His makeshift bandages were soaked with blood. Marcos' blood dried on my skin and clothing. The mixture of blood, sweat, and dirt ate into my wound. The pain of my wound increased over time. We were caught in a dilemma. We were trapped between two hostile masses, one on the far side of the bridge, and one in town. We were too weak to ride horses back to safety. However, we were safe for the moment, provided that we stayed in the barn. Moving and fighting was out of the question. Capture wasn't an option. I blacked out from the pain in my side and from the blistering heat in the barn. Nightfall approached us. Marcos regained new life. I could feel him nudging at my shoulder. "Mack, Mack, damnit, Mack wake up," Marcos said. I awoke from a deep sleep. I had hoped that this had just been a nightmare, but reality set in when I realized that we were still trapped inside the barn. Marcos had his back propped up against the wall. "I apologize that I got you into this mess," he said. "But you have to understand that Cortez had to be stopped. Many innocent people have died from his reign of tyranny. We were lucky to have an idiot like Carlos in charge. He kept Cortez in check. I believe that's why Cortez came to make sure the weapons were safe. Those weapons were for his own little Army. You see Cortez needed those weapons to support his conspiracy against Carlos. Ramos had nothing to do with the conspiracy. But anyway, I've got an idea to get us out of the shitty awful mess. If we stay, get captured, or run in to an ambush we die. However, there is one alternative that I'm pretty sure that Carlos men haven't thought of. Later tonight we walk back through town and board a cattle car back to Lascosis. There are number of reasons why this plan may work. Carlos' men wouldn't suspect us to walk back into the town that we fought so hard to get out of. They also probably think that we're dead. Cortez and Ramos are dead so there's no real leadership. But the main reason why I feel that this plan may work is that the remainder of Carlos' men have probably given up the idea of supporting the cause. They don't want to answer to Carlos. Think about it, no money, no weapons." We decided to try. We had no choice if we wanted to live.

That night at about midnight we entered the town after stealing the clothing off banditos who were left dead from our earlier conflict. All of the remaining banditos were either sleep or drunk. There was no more fight left in Carlos' men.

We hid in the cattle car, and the train left that morning to Brownsville. We linked back up with the Captain. This mission was over, and it turned out to be a complete success. Early the next morning the Captain summoned me for a debriefing. Out of the eight that started the mission, four remain alive. Marcos was the only operative that lived, but he would never fight again because his left arm was amputated. The Captain started his debriefing. "Gentlemen this mission was a complete success. Carlos and Ramos are dead. While Marcos and his team were in Monterey, our team was responsible for conducting surveillance on Carlos' activity back here. Our mission was to destroy the weapons if they made it back to Carlos. The weapons never made their way back to Lascosis. This action or might I say inaction brought distrust and discontent between Carlos and the Comencharos, resulting in a bloodbath between the two factions. The Comencharos were wiped out, and Carlos' second in command, Rodreuiez was mortally wounded. Carlos is on the run, and has gone into hiding. He is officially an outcast among his people. Eventually he'll be mopped up by local authorities. The President sends his personal thanks, but remember. This event never happened." Later that night I sat around sharing small talk with the Captain. He told me that a new movement was developing in the deep Southern part of Mexico. He said this movement was headed by a guy named Pucho Villa. However, he believed that this little problem had already been contained. It wasn't our problem anymore.

CHAPTER 9

LUCIFER'S DEN

My life, my emotions, and my spiritual stability, shifted in a new direction after that last mission. I understood that there's a thin line between the good and evil forces, and that the balance of life can be changed to death in a blink of an eye.

I never told the Captain what had actually happened back in Monterey. I felt that it was insignificant. I didn't want to tell him that he had been used by his old boss and friend. In any case, everything turned out okay. I believe that I was involved in one of the toughest counter espionage missions of the century. I wondered if there were any more agents like Marcos. Our unit was secret, but Marcos' unit had to be Washington's blackest secret. In order to be in a unit like that you had to be extremely fanatical, insane, or just completely naive.

I didn't see another mission again for another seven months. I had one year remaining in my contract. I had another birthday, and was now 19 years of age. All during spring, I enjoyed the small things I once took for granted. Spring was in full bloom. I'd take long hikes through the desert and observe the blooming of cactus flowers. The long sunsets were breathtaking and offered me a peace of mind. I understood why nobody in the unit ever talked about the missions. It didn't occur to me until one day when I had a moment of clarity during a blissful sunset. These missions brought out the real animals in men. This animal was ugly, uncompassionate, and extremely cold. This was a time of unrest, and when this unit was called to action, we were the surgeons who had to deal with the cancerous tumors of this hemisphere. That time of peace was meant for flushing our memories of the trash and filth that were gathered during the mission. This unit was to do the impossible. During this peaceful time, I made it imperative to live out every second of every day to its fullest. One day I woke up early to observe a sunrise. As sun rose from the east, a slight southern wind drifted in. There was something about feeling that southern wind and seeing the rising red sun. The truly gratifying experience came at dusk. I spent many nights on top of hills looking out at the vast brownish green desert watching that same big red disk settle in the western horizons. One late evening, I was returning from the range and I saw a group of scouts that had returned from some type of mission. It bothered me because I remembered that John, my old friend, had been was with this group. Immediately, a lump in my throat formed because I imagined the worst. I knew that they were not authorized to discuss their mission with me. I had a need to know what happened to my best friend. I had heard through the grapevine that John was being charged with treason. Hours later I hunted down Captain Faulkner to get information about John's alleged status. The Captain was in a somber mood. I knew that whatever happened was serious, because he invited me into his office and had me sit down and listen. He explained, "I want you to listen to me Mack. There's nothing that we can do to help John. John and a few of our scouts were assigned to the seventh Cavalry to aid in finding Geronimo. Allegedly John and another scout were out conducting a routine recon ahead of the main body. The commander of the unit became impatient with their patrolling techniques. When John had returned, the main body left on their own patrol. The ambitious Captain attacked a defenseless village of Navaho Indians. Women, children, and the defenseless elders were slaughtered. I knew this incompetent Captain personally, and in my opinion, this part of the story had to be true. The other scout that was with John told me that John became enraged at this gutless act. In retaliation, John led the unit directly into an Apache ambush that resulted in 30 dead soldiers, 18 mortally wounded, and captured horses. During the ambush, John allegedly crawled over to the Captain's position and blew his brains out. In the chaos, John evaded and escaped into the wilderness of the desert. To make matters worse, the Commanding General dispatched a platoon to capture John. Well, we both know that was stupid sending conventional soldiers after someone like John. That is like hunting a cat with a bunch of birds. John totally decimated the platoon, and never fired a shot. He made his message clear with his knife. The C.G. called off the hunt and turned this problem over to the local authorities. Like I said Mack, there's nothing that can be done to help John." Unfortunately, John ended up in the wrong place, at the wrong time, with the wrong mission. The grotesque reality about this business is that it could have happened to anyone of us in this type of unit.

After a well deserved six months of vacation, my skills needed to be sharpened. Thus, my remaining free time was spent at the rifle range. I had recovered mentally and physically from the Carlos mission. I had a new motivation. I had under one year in my contract. I still had a true love for my unit, but the stakes were too high. Just as everything was almost going well, I was put on alert once again. I was to report for a warning order once again at Captains Faulkner's house.

As usual, the briefing room was covered with maps, pictures, and concept sketches. The smell of freshly brewed coffee and cigar smoke filled the air. The biggest change that I noticed was that audience population had increased and there were many new faces, which meant that the Faulkner had tailor-fitted this mission with a wide range of skills. The room was filled to standing room only. Judging by the pictures and the maps, this mission was to take place somewhere in South Carolina. Before I had an opportunity to pinpoint the exact location, the briefing began. This time the Captain wasn't all smiles and grins. He had a stony expression on his face and an unyielding jaw. When he began to speak, his nostrils flared. "Gentlemen, this mission is unlike any mission that I have ever encountered. There's a town located north of Savannah, Georgia that needs a total realignment. This town has been operating on its own set of rules for a while. These rules aren't about life, liberty, and the pursuit of happiness. Instead these rules include murder, deceit, and many other lawless actions. You know as well as I that when a crises like this develops, it spreads like wildfire. So far the President believes that this diseased growth is localized to one particular area. But the real problem is that the origin has been difficult to detect. This is a highly sensitive mission, because it involves a conspiracy plot at the highest levels of political office. However, we have a starting point. The idea is to make an example of our starting point. Our ability to turn around this lawless town should have a domino effect on others that are following this lawless role model. The local authorities haven't done anything, because the law in this region is part of this conspiracy. We are to start our cleansing in the town of Buford, South Carolina. This town has reached an epic proportion of anarchy," he explained.

The Captain passed out pictures for everyone. He paused and allows everyone to soak up the picture. The photo was an old black and white photo taken during the civil war of a Cavalry officer. "This is retired Lieutenant Colonel Bloody Jack McDowell. He commanded a unit during the civil war called the Missouri Rough Riders. He was a real maverick among the circle of officers. He was obsessive and became a fanatic of the old south's beliefs. His main targets were then, and today, are aimed at people that don't believe what he believes. During the war he committed many atrocities. After the war he was prosecuted for committing violent crimes against humanity. Somehow, his wealth and influence got him exonerated and now he is a territorial judge in South Carolina. It's ironic how some of the people that he sentenced are now a part of his payroll. He's back to his old tricks, but this time learned how to cover up his mess. He has the wealth and the means to do as he pleases. Who's gonna prosecute him? He's a political giant in the territory. His financial status gives him the leverage to control whomever, whatever, and whenever he desires. For about two months his activity has been secretly monitored, however, efforts had failed until about one week ago. We have a witness that is alive and well. He's our guest speaker in our phase two of this briefing. Also, apparently there are some decent people of this town that are underground who wanted this problem eliminated. Lately McDowell has found out that that there was a partition against him. In response to this leak, he has unleashed a reign of terror of epic proportion. We've been told that he has lined up shop owners, bankers, and many of the business owners in the streets and shot them dead. He replaced those businesses with his people. To insure that nobody speaks against him, he's killed entire families. He owns the town and people are afraid to speak against him. He basically holds the town hostage. He controls the economic growth of the region. McDowell's assets include the largest cotton mills, cattle business, and internal infrastructure. For his personal protection, he has 40 to 50 loyal gunmen that he sentenced as a judge. They are personally indebted to accomplishing McDowell's illegal and demented goals. There are four close associates that assist with McDowell's command and control functions." The Captain passed out pictures of each man and continued his briefing in stride. "The first guy is Charley Babb from Texas. He's known for shooting people in the back, and is very shady about eliminating resistance. He is believed to be McDowell's cleanup man. He's responsible for cleaning up all illegal activity that McDowell conducts. He is well educated and hold a law degree. The next man is Henry Ambrose an exlawman from Kansas who was kicked out of the state for using excessive force on cattlemen and ranchers. He achieved his wealth by taking protection money from citizens of the town. The third man is Cecil Radford, McDowell's close cousin. He disappeared for three years after successfully robbing a bank in Boston. He allegedly gunned down three bank tellers, and two female bystanders. He has resurfaced as one of McDowell's boys. Finally, the most dangerous of the bunch is Kenneth Merriweather from New Orleans, an ex-riverboat gambler and licensed accountant. He kept McDowell's books straight and legal. He's also the fastest gunman in the territory, and has 10 confirmed kills under his belt."

For the next few hours, the Captain entertained questions about the current situation in Buford. He hadn't briefed us about on how we were to execute this mission. He was saving that for phase three of his briefing. He also wanted to make sure that everyone understood what they were up against. We broke for lunch and returned late in the evening for phase two of the briefing.

There were 32 of us at phase two of the briefing. We were all sitting around the campfire ready to listen to our star witness. I didn't want to hear about the suffering and carnage because it was all too similar to the Carlos mission, it was part of the briefing, so I had to listen. The Captain escorted an old man to us. His face was wrinkled and his hair was pure white. He looked to be 75 or 80 years old. He walked with a limp and his eyes were deep inside his shadowy facial features.

The wind was calm, and the moon was full. The area was illuminated as if it were daylight.

The area got quiet as he made his way into our assembly area. The only thing we heard were his limp as he dragged leaves that were in his path. He began to talk in stride as he approached us. His speech was broken, and he spoke in a monotone voice. "You fellows gonna kill the white devil? Kill all those sons of bitches who's with him because they're are cursed. I'm gonna tell you a true story that happened a week ago." His anger began to surface as he got deeper into his story. "After the big war, I moved my family to a black settlement outside of Buford. After three good years of sharecropping with the plantation owners, our town began to prosper. We cultivated the land until the soil was fertile and rich. Our village bought cattle to become self-supportive. Both of my sons and their families grew up here. The community began to grow. At the time, Buford hadn't expanded, and the surrounding neighborhoods were undeveloped. Then one day the mayor and McDowell showed up in our village. The mayor was all smiles and handshakes, but McDowell kept to himself and stayed distant. After an hour of touring our boundaries, they returned, however, the mayor had an attitude adjustment. All I could hear was "nigger this" and "nigger that." McDowell was laughing and kicking the kids that were around the buggy. The mayor left in a total outrage. Last week gunmen rode into our village and were confronted by our councilman. Whatever they said seemed to upset our councilman. Later that night, we had a mandatory town meeting at the church. The message that was supposed to be relayed was that we had one week to move off this property and settle elsewhere out of the state. The councilman proposed that we move for the safety of our families. Within twenty minutes into our meeting McDowell's henchmen appeared from all directions. They didn't even bother about masking themselves. Bullets began to penetrate through the church's thin walls. I tried to dodge bullets, but I kept tripping over the dead bodies of people. Everyone was hugging the ground trying to get cover. Children were crying, women were screaming but it didn't matter to those murdering savages. A few moments later I smelled smoke. The thugs had lit the building on fire. There was a large explosion. I must have been knocked out, because I don't remember what happened after the explosion. I woke up burried beneath the rubble. I couldn't move. All I could do is watch. I still have nightmares at the heinous act that I saw. As an added protective measure the thugs went around to all of the bodies and shot them to make sure that there were no witnesses. When I thought it was over, the butchers dug a mass grave, piled all the dead bodies in the grave, and poured kerosene on the bodies and set a torch to them. McDowell was there laughing and drinking as if it was some type of party. Later, they covered the dead with dirt. It was a total wholesale destruction. They finished the job by burning down the remaining homes in the village." The old man began to cry. He left our assembly area crying.

Captain Faulkner interrupted our moment of grief. "Some of the dead children were found later. McDowell and Charley Babb covered it up by scalping them to make it look like it was an attack from the Indians. I believe that eventually this excuse will be used as a means to expand McDowell's wealth onto the reservation. McDowell is smart, influential, and extremely dangerous. Gentlemen, now you see what we are up against. I'm sure that the situation in Buford is much more worse than what we've heard. Tomorrow morning I will brief phase three of this operation."

That night my mind ran amak as I lie in bed. The first thing that came to mind, was how this briefing was set up compared to the Carlos brief. The Carlos briefing lasted a few hours. This briefing was so long that it was broken down into phases. The Carlos briefing didn't include a witness. We only had eight men to go against many for the Carlos mission. This time we had over thirty men to go against fewer men. The complexity of this mission hit me in my gut. There were more clouded variables that hadn't been addressed. The intangibles worried me. Carlos' mission was chalked with intangibles. I couldn't sleep because I kept thinking about the mission. I rolled onto my stomach, hoping that that position would offer me comfort, but the roast beef that I had eaten for dinner hadn't settle quite right. I rolled to my side and I thought about how luck was on my side at the last mission. It seem to me that this mission was much more complex. Unfortunately, I felt that luck wouldn't be enough, "I need an edge," I whispered. But not an edge like weapons, bullets, or any of the material tools. These were just multipliers. I needed an edge in a spiritual sense. Something that couldn't be seen or heard, but could be felt. I needed to be able to project a dominating presence. I believed that this mission would call for a lot of interfacing with the enemy. Flashbacks of the gunfight with Carlos' men entered my mind. I could feel their inner anxiety. After the Carlos mission, I was a veteran. I definitely believed that I had learned from that mission that adaptation would be the key to my survival. I remembered the story about gazelle's ability to adapt and survive in a jungle full of predators. This mission was definitely in a jungle. But who's the predator and who's the prey? I wondered. I was tired but I couldn't sleep.

Phase three of the briefing was started the next morning at 0600 at the Captain Faulkner house inside his den. This time there were no maps or concept sketches. Faulkner saw me looking around for the missing maps and other paraphernalia, so he immediately addressed this issue. "Gentlemen this is the conclusion of the briefings. After phase three we began phase four of this operation." I had no idea that there were more phases to this operation. Faulkner continued, "You men noticed that there are no map, concept sketches, or even pictures. These tools aren't needed because this mission is about an idea. This mission has no known physical objective. This conflict is about gaining a physiological advantage. My directives are to expose McDowell's illegal operations and to disrupt his powerbase by whatever means. It is believed that when we accomplish these directives, McDowell's empire will crumble. Once the current regime is neutralized, a legitimate city government must be restored. I can assure you that this mission will not be a cake walk. Like I said, this mission doesn't require a map. Hell, Buford is easy to find. And anyone can just go and arrest McDowell anytime. The issue is changing people's southern ideology that has been implanted for so long. Our mission's essential task is to gain control of the town immediately. So, when we ride into town we'll close every business down, declare martial law, and implement a curfew. That means that we'll have to wear our uniforms. The uniforms will create the illusion that the government is in charge. This will demonstrate to the people that we are in charge and not McDowell. The principle allies for this mission will be surprise and balance. Each one of us must keep this principle in mind because these elements are the foundation for this mission. I am hoping that he'll try something stupid initially. He'll have no idea what he's up against. But I think that he's smarter than that. We'll make our headquarters in the center balance of the town, which I believe to be the courthouse that is next to the town jail. By then if we don't get the desired response, I'll take it to the next step. We simply go out in the community and pick a fight. We can't allow our actions to become stagnant. Meanwhile, we'll continue to apply pressure by enforcing strict alcohol and gambling laws and put a strain on McDowell's financial resources such as the town stores and his banking industry. There's no way to anticipate the moves of McDowell or the townspeople, so it would be impossible for me to draw up some type of battle plan. Therefore we must be able to improvise and be imaginative. At no time can we allow the situation to control us. We control the situation. In their eyes we're the bad guys, because our action will be aggressive in nature, and ruthless at times. However, we must operate within the confines of the law. Remember this when you think that we may be a little overzealous: These people voted McDowell into office. Gentlemen the train leaves for Savannah tonight. We'll initially prepare our gear at Fort Pellaski, Georgia. From this point on we're not to discuss this mission with anyone."

As I walked back to the barracks, my pessimistic side took over. I thought that this might be the last time that I'd be taking this walk to the barracks. I thought, what if this mission blew up in our faces? I remembered that Marcos and I barely made it through the last mission. I could see Faulkner's perplexed feeling about this mission. I decided that I'd better fit myself with everything and every weapon in my personal arsenal. As I packed my arsenal, the optimistic side of me began to surface. I cleaned and holstered my 45 and 44 pistols, carried two additional shoulder holstered 45 pistols. I placed a derringer in the left sleeve of my boot, and mounted two loaded sawed off double barreled shotguns on my horse. I cleaned my 30.06 rifle and bore scoped my rifle scoped, and packed it away. I broke down my sharps sniper rifle into two components and placed it in my velvet made case, loaded as much ammunition as I could and mounted it on my horse. I figured that having all these weapons at my disposal would increase the chances of becoming a living civilian someday soon. I didn't want do die in that town. These weapons leveled the playing field.

5 July 1876 0200

After traveling for about two days, we arrived in Savanna incognito. We rode our horses like ghost in the wind and arrived at Fort Pullaski two hours later. The fort was a temporary stop. We didn't stay very long. Before activity in the fort started, we were long gone out of the front gate. We rode along the eastern coast as a guide to Buford. That night we camped on the beach 30 miles south of Buford. That night I couldn't sleep because I was becoming obsessed with the mission. Consequently, I decided to take a stroll down the beach seawall. It was a beautiful night. The half moon illuminated the gargantuan Atlantic. The low tidal wave from the ocean drifted in and out, leaving a fresh-smelling mist. I sat down in awe listening to the waves. It was so quiet...quiet.... I drifted into an inner peace with myself as if I was meditating. Footsteps moved in my direction. I turned around. It was Captain Faulkner. He couldn't sleep either.

"Mack, is that you sitting out there?" Faulkner called out.

I answered, "Yes sir, it's me." He approached me and shook my hand.

"Congratulations, Staff Sergeant Mack. I never got to tell you that you've been promoted to the rank of Sergeant First Class. Marcos told me the whole story behind the Carlos mission. I have to say, job well done. You are officially the second in command."

I reshook Faulkner's hand, "Thank you sir." I decided to ask, "What's your true gut feeling about this mission?" The Captain looked at me with a half grin, because I think he knew that I didn't care about any promotion, and he replied, "I don't register a feeling, and that's what bothers me. This mission is clouded with deceit, conspiracy, and contempt. I believe that Buford is the tip of the iceberg. In my opinion McDowell is the tail end of the bull. The million dollar question is who is McDowell's boss? McDowell has stepped over the line and we are supposed to conduct a silent and secret quick fix on someone else's mistake. That's why I pulled out all the stops in this mission. I don't know what to expect when we ride into Buford. The only thing I know is what we're capable of doing. I have no real idea of what McDowell is capable of doing, and that's my dilemma. McDowell is a powerful man, but his boss has become scared or envious of McDowell's fame to power. He has become self-sufficient and his operation grows larger as we speak. I don't have any idea on what we're facing."

Faulkner and I went over a few details about the mission for the rest of the night. If Faulkner was there to comfort my anxiousness about this mission, he failed miserably.

My new rank and responsibilities changed my outlook on how I would conduct myself. Perhaps Captain Faulkner saw something in me that I didn't see in myself. All I knew was that I had better be prepared to perform when the time came. I had so many questions about this mission, but not enough answers. I was put in charge of the Quartering party. My mission was to leave ahead of the main body and set up an assembly position in the vicinity of the massacre site. We had the responsibility to secure the site by using cordon and search techniques, and block entry and exit points that lead into the area. We were also to link up with an undercover operative that had been in Buford for a long time. The Captain and I had no idea who this operative was, or what he looked like. Once the Assembly area had been established, the Captain would bring in the main body.

6 July 1878 0400

My quartering party left that morning at 0400. I could tell that today was going to another typical summer day. The humidity had already set in before dawn. As we approached the swamps, the mosquitoes swarmed around us. At 0700 hours we reached our proposed assembly site. The skeletal remains of the village, the odor of burnt wood, and the foundations of buildings were outlined by charred bricks. There were no furniture, toys, or clothing in the area. There were no other human beings within the scope of our operational area. The village was surrounded by deep woods.

Once the site was secured, we conducted our internal patrolling of the area. After posting security at the exit and entry points, myself and three others decided to find the mass grave site. At about noon, we ran into a small clearing that was surrounded by trees. The ground around this area was soft and the dirt had been freshly dug. I knew then that we found the mass grave site. I didn't bother digging up the area. I just didn't have the stomach. We rode back to the command post and waited for Faulkner and the Operative. Later that evening at about 1400 hours Corporal David Walker reported that he made contact with a man who told him that he was looking for a silver mine. He had left him under guard at the outpost. I realized that the Corporal had made contact with the operative. Silver mine was the code word. I immediately went to the outpost. I approached the operative. He was a tall, slightly obese white man that stood 6'3". He wore a heavy beard and his blue eyes sunk deep into his head. He was carrying a side arm on his right hip and a machete on his left. I issued him with the challenge, "I understand that you're looking for silver."

He responded with the password, "Silver can always be found in Dallas Texas. Jonathan Stone, pleased to meet you." The operative held out his hand.

"Sergeant First Class Mack. Pleased to meet you." We firmly gripped hands and shook, however, once again I felt skeptical about his agenda. Still, I welcomed him over to the C.P. We sat down after I poured him a cup of coffee. The operative took out a large chew of tobacco and stuffed it into his mouth. He handed me a chunk and I did the same. The operative immediately started to explain his current situation. "You're gonna have to relay this information to your boss because I've got to get back before they suspect anything." We had plenty of time so I listened to the operative's story. The operative wiped the sweat off his brow and told his story in detail.

"My primary mission was to gather information that would convict or lead to the conviction of Black Jack McDowell. My second objective was to uncover or expose any operation affiliated with McDowell's enterprise. My cover is the town drunk. One month ago, I drifted into Buford as a stagecoach attendant. Once the stage coach made its normal stop from Charleston to here, I staged a fight with the stagecoach master. He fired me on the spot. A day later I made friends with the saloon manager of the Winking Lizard Saloon. Over a period of two days I ran my tab over the amount that I could pay. I gave people in the town the illusion that I had a drinking problem, and that I really didn't pose a threat. My wit and humor helped me inch my way within the community. I got trickles of information through the bottle, but nothing that was significant. Then one day the break that I was looking for appeared. A black family of settlers rode into town one day to water their horses. They were unaware of the type of people that lived here. Unfortunately for them, Charley Babb and two of his hoodlums were also in the area. I had to act fast, because Charley and his boys had honed in on the unsuspecting family. I quickly jumped in the street to stop their progress. The unsuspecting father of the family jumped off the wagon to shake my hand in a friendly gesture. I greeted him with a punch to the stomach and a right upper cut to the jaw. Crowds began to gather in the streets in order to watch this spectacle. I carried on this act until I got the response that I was hoping for. The mass of town's people began to rant and cheer about this demonstration of pure bigotry. Finally, the family left just as they entered. The town sheriff came over to me and offered me a drink. From that moment on, I became one of the boys. Just as I was downing my second drink Charley Babb and his boys congratulated me and bought more drinks. I continued to lure them in with jovial attitude and jokes. After about eight more shots of whiskey I had won a substantial amount of credibility with Charley. After all he enjoyed liquor and laughter. I decided that I had to leave because alcohol and trying to conduct a secret mission don't mix. As I was leaving the Winking Lizard Saloon, in a surge of elation Charley stopped me and said, 'hey man you want a job to pay off your damn whiskey tab. I don't know what the hell that you're qualified to do. If you don't take the job I'll pay your whiskey tab off with your ass.' Charley got serious and pulled out his pistol and aimed it at me. The saloon got quiet, and the music stopped playing. We looked at each other and like a volcano I involuntarily spewed vomit everywhere. The entire saloon went into a complete laughing rage. Charley responded swelling with laughter, 'I see what you're qualified to do, you're the fastest puking asshole on this side of the Mississippi.' He holstered his weapon and we both staggered our way out of the saloon. Finally, I was inside of McDowell's organization. We drunkenly stumbled our way towards the town church. 'Where the hell are we going, Charley?' 'We're going to meet your new boss. And don't throw up on him.' 'Don't worry Charley I'll dazzle him when I shit in my britches,' I responded in laughter. We entered the church, and Charley pointed him out to me, 'There he is, he's behind the pulpit.'

I thought 'there he is, Lucifer live and in color.' There was nothing normal about this guy, so he was easy to spot. In fact he gave me the creeps. I was amazed with his attire because he was flamboyantly dressed for the winter months. He wore a large black overcoat, light gray baggy pants stuffed in his black spit polished Hessian style boots. His hair was wet and plastered back hung down to his shoulders, but the most noticeable thing about his hair was that it was pure white, as if it had been bleached. He had thick shabby white eyebrows that overlapped his eye-sockets. His skin was pale and wrinkled. Bottom line, McDowell is one ugly son of a bitch. It was like I was looking at an embalmed corpse. I had to stop staring because I was beginning to feel squeamish. After I gathered my faculties, I realized that this couldn't be a spiritual gathering on a Tuesday night. The money basket was being passed around. I noticed that large dollar bills were being placed in the basket by his well-dressed audience. I realized then that these business people were paying McDowell's protection fee. He uses this assembly of God as a cover to do his evil bidding. I was in total awe by this sight. Now that I'm under McDowell's payroll I've been able to piece bits of information together about McDowell. Sergeant Mack, I'm telling you this information in detail because you need to fully understand what you're up against. McDowell is a control freak. He wears many hats. He is the self-appointed Mayor of Buford. His primary job had been territorial judge. He received his law degree from Harvard, therefore he might be insane but he's smart. He achieved his wealth by birth right. His father owned two of the largest cotton mills in the state, and lived in one of the largest mansions in the south. The civil war brought hard times to the McDowells. The slaves that worked the fields were freed, leaving the cotton business to go bankrupt. Old man McDowell died of a heart attack when he found out that his land and business were being confiscated as part of the war reparations act, but the nail that put the old man in the coffin was that his son Black Jack McDowell had been captured by a Black unit in Savannah. To make this story short, somehow he legally acquired most of his wealth back, and now he blames the colored race for the past. A year ago a friend of mine was mysteriously killed while investigating a organized group that rose from the ashes of the civil war called the S.S.W.P. or Secret Society of White People. Their goal is to restore the old southern traditions. Clean this country of all foreigners. This group is composed of people in high places such as government officials, judges, lawyers, doctors, and many wealthy land owners. This group is dangerous, because they are well educated and have money. They are hard to get because they keep it secret. Well anyway, McDowell is linked with this organization. He's become a threat to this secret society, because of his aggressive behavior. He's got a real choke hold on Buford. McDowell is a major stockholder of Buford County National Bank. He has strategically implanted his people inside of the businesses, to keep an inside edge over the owners. McDowell's true strength lies in the amount of men that are under his payroll. He has 25 to 40 gunmen under his payroll. I provided McDowell security at his so called church sessions. I sat through most of his court sessions and provided security at most of his menial jobs. By working all of these odd jobs, I pieced together how his security structure is set up. He had three groups of security. Advancement to the next group or level is based on merit. The first group is the general support group. This is my current level. This General Support level is the largest group. The number of men fluctuate on a weekly basis, but it ranges from 16 to 25. The second level does the real damage. At this level you conduct raids and most of the illegal activity. This level is mainly offensive in nature. The members at this level have been with McDowell for a long period of time. Most of these members were recruited by McDowell's primary staff. Currently there are 18 members in this group. The next level of security is the group that is the most secret level of the groups. Everything that I know about this group is based on hearsay. These members are like McDowell's secret police. This level is like the counter-intelligence group. The spies come from this group. No one knows how large this group is except for McDowell. This group is McDowell's ace in the hole. The first level is there mainly to earn a paycheck. This level is the least committed group. Some leave immediately after they receive their first paycheck. Most of these members live in town. Then once you make it to the second level, there's no way out. You're in for life. This level is committed to McDowell. This group is the strong arm of McDowell. These members are housed at McDowell's place. The third level are the true fanatics. They believe and support McDowell in a spiritual sense. These guys are mystic but highly dangerous because they will die for the cause if necessary. It is unknown where these people live. I'm not sure if I am destined for fame and fortune or obscurity and vagueness. It was initially difficult to break into this organization and gather information, however, now that I got my foot in the door, information comes at me at an alarming rate. This mission has forced me to throw away my many years of training on information gathering. I have stumbled my way of obtaining information. One day I was responsible for providing security for Judge McDowell during a court hearing. He asked me to run back to his office and get his swearing in Bible that was located on his desk. I rushed to his office, picked up the Bible, and clumsily dropped it to the ground. As I was attempting to pick up the good book, I glanced at one of the pages. This book was no Bible, but a Bible cover covered the outside. The inside pages were filled with names and addresses. This had to be McDowell's contacts. I didn't have time to look at the names because Charley Babb walked into the room. Charley took the book away from me and gave me a suspicious look. Immediately I said to him, 'the Judge asked me to fetch this book.' Charley looked at me with suspicious bewilderment and responded, 'I'll deliver this to his majesty.' If you guys expect to implicate and uncover this conspiracy, that book is the key. From that day on, Charley has kept a close eye on my activity. Finally, my commitment to McDowell's allegiance would be tested. Charley and I were finishing off a fifth of whiskey in the Winking Lizard saloon. Charley said to me, 'I think that you are ready to take the next step.'

'What the hell are you talking about Charley?' I responded.

'The boss is having us to raid a nigger town tonight,' Charley answered. If Charley saw me hesitate, my cover would had been blown.

'Charley, you mean we gonna waste a good set of bullets on a bunch of niggers?' 'Hell yeah, count me in,' I jokingly answered. This wasn't a raid. A raid is conducted in order to gather information, destroy, or capture the enemy. This event was a pure genocidal cleansing. I was stuck between a rock and a hard place. I had to participate or blow my cover. Innocent men, women, and children were raided and massacred. I will have to remember this intolerable act for the remainder of my life. My level of existence with these people has reached a new low. The whole time Charley Babb kept his eyes on me. After the slaughter was over,

Charley's job is the sweep. As the sweeper he's responsible for clearing evidence. As I was sifting through the debris I found a survivor. It was an old man that had been knocked unconscious. I woke him up and told him to lay still until we swept the area. I told him to make his way to Fort Pullaski, and report what had happened here. I assumed that he escaped the area, because when I came back he was gone. And now I am part of McDowell's second level of security. Sergeant Mack that's all I know about McDowell's operation. I have to leave soon because Charley may become suspicious of my whereabouts. Please insure the Captain knows what I told you here today."

1700 that evening

I watched the operative ride into the woods until he was out of sight. I had no idea that he would be bringing that amount of detailed information to the table. I was under the impression that his information would be composed of abstract elements, however, his information substantiated what Captain Faulkner was talking about. We were not fighting against a known physical enemy. We were fighting against something that couldn't be seen or heard. We were fighting against idea. I thought, how could someone dream up a sick demented notion such as the one in Buford, and follow through on it like McDowell has been doing? I also couldn't believe how complicated the operative had become. It seemed to me that he was being smothered by his surroundings. And now that he had been accepted into the second level of McDowell's family, I wondered how much longer he could swim without being drowned by the environment. I knew that Captain Faulkner would try to get that book, but I wondered how, and where McDowell would keep that book? Faulkner arrived two hours after the operative had left. I briefed him on what the operative had reported. Late that evening the team met with Faulkner to once again reinforce and readjust the plan according to the new information that was given by the operative. Faulkner seemed confident at this large task and commented, "Remember gentlemen, balance is the key. Think of this mission like a pendulum that swings back and forth. Currently, the pendulum has already shifted to the side of McDowell. The idea is to shift the pendulum on our side by whatever means. We will be spread thin throughout Buford. There is unstableness about this mission. I cannot predict how the town will react. There will be time that you will have to take a risk. There'll be times that you'll be working independent but remember this, whatever you do, conduct it with passion and resolve. If you have to strike, strike hard and deep. If you have to fight, fight to win. If you have to shoot, shoot to kill. At no time can you show apprehension. Gentlemen, this is untraveled territory. There are no book answers, there's just actions and reactions. This time men, we'll be the bad guys through the eyes of the citizens. I stand here on the graves of the innocent that suffered at the hands of McDowell's greed. Force will be met with stiffer force. With this idea in mind, the plan is simple. We'll close off the town, choke off the resources, shake the town up, and see what drops out."

Captain Faulkner had given us free reign to impose our wills against the wills of those that supported McDowell, and there's one rule to follow, and that rule was that there were no rules. There were a couple of key essential points that had to be occupied such as observational points that had to be manned with snipers. In addition, the court house and sheriff's office had to be captured, and later McDowell's home had to be raided.

This mission also represented my last mission. After this mission, I was planning to buy some land and start a family farming business. I knew deep in my heart that it was imperative that I got out before my soul hardened. I could feel that I was transforming into something cold and ruthless. I had to quit soon before I became an empty shell. As it stood I had the ability to contain the beast within me. Finally, I dozed off into a deep sleep.

0330 early morning 7 July 1878

There was a gentle nudge on my shoulder, "Wake up, it's show time," Faulkner said softly. I quickly gathered my gear and went through my ritual of preparing my weapons of death. Our unit assembled together prior to moving out. I looked around at the men to conduct a brief last minute inspection. I realized that wasn't really necessary because everyone in this unit was expert. We were supposed to look like a normal conventional army unit. Instead everyone was packing their weapon of choice. In any case, the uniforms became a moot point because most of us had put on the long overcoat type rain gear. It never occurred to me until now. I wondered how many men were actually in this unit. I mounted my horse that was positioned next to Faulkner and asked him, "Sir, I was just wondering, since you're here and Sergeant McCish has retired, who's in charge of the rest of the men back at Fort Sill?"

The Captain looked at me with a smiled and responded, "This is it. What you see here today is the whole unit. There are no replacements, there is no back up, it's just us and the God almighty."

The air was dry, and the moon couldn't be seen because thick cumulus clouds blanketed the sky. There was a distant rumbling of thunder from the east. A storm front was coming in from the South, moving in a Northwesterly direction out of the Atlantic Ocean. The wind picked up and blew in from the southeast. The thick fog that collected in the area had blown out of the area. Like the distant storm that was moving in, we moved out with the same tenacity. The stiff wind was at our backs, thus the ride was fast. Like clockwork, riders automatically separated from the massive body of avenging angels in order to move into their blocking positions. Finally the massive body stopped on a ridge located just above the city limits. We had a clear shot of the town that sat in the valley. The Captain's intent was to allow the observation point people time to move into position. The Captain and I took out our binoculars to see if we could see any activity in the streets, but there was none. A dismal thought crossed my mind as I looked at the empty streets. Could this be an ambush like the Carlos mission? I guess we were at the point of no return. This mission is a go. Ambush or not, we moved out. Just as we were closing in on the town, sheets of rain hammered into everything. The dusty streets turned into a quagmire of mud. Our momentum was too great for the natural elements to slow our progress. Pure adrenaline was pumping through my veins. This occupation would either be a total surprise or a total slaughter. In either case, we were going to find out soon. We stopped in front of the sheriff's office and dismounted. While I dismounted, our men sprinted into their strategic position. The Captain, three other soldiers and I awaited outside the door of the sheriff's office while waiting for everyone to fall into position. A minute passed and it was our turn to make our move. The three soldiers that were with the command group didn't bother to knock. They just kicked in the door. Two deputies that were on duty were caught in a dead sleep. One was dressed in his long underwear. "What the hell!" the deputy said loudly. The deputies looked at us as if they had seen a ghost. The deputy that was dressed responded, "Damn, hoodwinked by a bunch of nig," and before the idiot finished his sentence I hammered my rifle-butt into his ribs. He folded over onto the floor, and I walked over to him and said "Oh, I'm sorry. And you were saying?" Shortly afterwards they were thrown into separate jail cells. Our next move was to take control of the town's center balance; city hall. This is where we'd find all land transactions and property deeds. We busted into the town hall with no incidents. We put pad locks on the door. We repeated the same for all of the big businesses except for the saloon.

After this task was completed we posted guards. Dusk was right around the corner. Meanwhile Captain Faulkner had already awakened the new mayor and escorted him to the jail. The mayor was in total consternation at the events that were unfolding. I watched Faulkner explain the rules to the mayor. The mayor frantically looked at Faulkner, and then he looked at me. "Mr. Mayor, your town is now under federal jurisdiction. My orders are to investigate various hate crimes committed by you and your good citizens of Buford. The charges range from murder, treason, conspiracy, jaywalking, picking your nose, and anything I can uncover about this God forsaken dump of a town. And you, mayor asshole, will be the first person that I'll investigate. Mack lock up this piece of shit," Faulkner angrily said. I grabbed the mayor by his shirt collar and he resisted. The mayor furiously cried out, "What's the charges?"

I interrupted and said, "Resisting arrest." I continued to push him towards the jail cell, and again he resisted and rudely said,

"Keep your black fucking paws off of me, damn nigger." The mayor triggered the beast within me. I ferociously began to beat him. I hammered the mayor with my fist. By the time Faulkner pulled me off the mayor, he was bleeding from every orifice. I threw him in the jail cell with the deputy that I whipped. I felt relaxed after that episode. I felt a sense of relaxation after each beating. It was like working out years of frustration and humiliation. Somehow I think Faulkner had enjoyed these ass whipping events. I looked at Faulkner as I was wiping the mayor's blood off my hands and asked, "Alright boss, who's next?" Faulkner's plan to divide and conquer was easy to follow. Out of the blue, he looked at his watch and said, "Ok, Mack, McDowell should be arriving soon."

I looked at my watch and then looked outside. It was 0600 and the daylight had come into view. I remembered that McDowell was an early riser. We briskly moved into hiding positions. We sterilized the area to give the appearance that everything was business as usual. I asked Faulkner prior to moving into my hide position, "Sir what about the pad locks." Captain Faulkner looked around and saw most of the businesses had been padlocked. There was little to no time to unlock all the buildings, and Faulkner didn't want to jeopardize the element of surprise. A decision had to be made. Reports from the observation post had begun to filter in. Some of the business owners were making their way to open up their businesses. Suddenly Sergeant Franklin, positioned in the church tower, received a report that was relayed from Observation Point 2 via hand and arm signals. Franklin yelled down to Faulkner, "Sir, Op2 reports that McDowell is one mile out and on his way into town."

Faulkner looked over to me with an annoyed look and says, "There's no time. Leave the locks and hope the hell that McDowell don't see them and let the shop-owners think that it's McDowell's trick. Confusion will be our ally. Once the shop-owners and McDowell try to sort out what's going on, we'll move in and take McDowell." I smiled at the Captain because I was amazed at how quickly he could analyze his situation and come up with a plan. I quickly moved into the corner alley between the jail and the courthouse. Faulkner moved back into the sheriff's office.

Minutes later, James Roberts, the owner of the town's General Store, and Lance Fieldler, the town's bank manager, tried to open the doors to their business but were unsuccessful. Three others showed up and had the same results. The owners met in the middle of the street to voice their frustrations. Captain Faulkner was right. The owners thought that this was just another ploy of McDowell.

Suddenly McDowell showed up with two of his heavily armed henchmen. They stopped and dismounted in front of the sheriff's office. The shop owners crowded around McDowell to voice their displeasure. Suddenly I saw McDowell throw his arm in disgust, yelling, "I didn't close a damn thing." That event triggered the Captain to walk out of the sheriff's office, which triggered us to move out of the shadows, and in for the kill. The Captain approached the crowd. All ten of us approached the crowd from different directions. We approached the crowd, guns locked and cocked at the ready position.

Captain Faulkner directed his attention on McDowell and said to him in a contemptuous tone, "Mr. McDowell it's an honor to meet you. On behalf of the decent citizens of United States, black, white, Indian and other, you're under arrest." I walked out of the shadows with my double barreled shotgun in the ready position. McDowell was in the middle of the shop owners, and his guards were still mounted on their horses. One of McDowell's guards flinched as if he was going for his weapon. I reacted and blew the guard off his horse. The group of shop owners and McDowell watched in horror as the corpse lay on the ground with a gunshot wound deeply imbedded in his chest. Blood and flesh had splashed on the crowd. I quickly reloaded and approached McDowell. The shop owners backed out of the way and opened up a lane, leaving McDowell isolated. McDowell stood his ground. While approaching McDowell, I asked his petrified followers, "I speak in behalf of this double barrel shotgun. Who's next?"Our eyes converged. McDowell and I stared at each other. I pointed the smoking barrels at his head, lips pursed with suppressed fury and said in a low monotone voice to McDowell, "Flinch a muscle, twitch an eye, or scratch your ass. Please give me an excuse to blow your sorry ass to hell." McDowell was no fool, he knew that I would deliver my promise of death. Captain Faulkner intervened, speaking to McDowell, "Hey asshole if you're not ready to meet your maker, you'd better come with me. We have a lovely bunch of fellows in your nice facility jail house. It awaits your sorry presence."

The Captain's plan worked so far. Most of the executive board had been locked up. The town was sealed so nobody could enter or exit. At 0700 civilians had began to crowd the streets. Our presence could be seen. Mid morning had passed and people had begun to gather in bunches. It was a strange sight to people ignoring our guards. They looked at them as if they were a part of the town. The only ones that showed a concern about the guards were the kids, and they were amazed at the uniforms. Little by little, frustrated shop owners would stand around their businesses wondering why they were closed. Faulkner and I sat in the sheriff's office playing a game of poker.

A thought occurred to me. I showed Faulkner a royal flush and asked, "Captain Faulkner, have you seen the sheriff yet?"

Faulkner showed signs of anger at defeat at our game, and angrily responded, "You lucky bastard. No I ain't seen hide nor hair of the sheriff. I'll deal this time." After whipping the Captain in poker, at 2100 hours I got up to see what had developed in the streets. I looked out the window and saw that the small groups of shop-owners had grown in size. I ask the Captain Faulkner, "Sir, what do you propose to do about our pad locks?" Faulkner was composed and content with the current situation.

He answered with confidence, "The only thing that those shop owners have got to do is walk right in this office and ask us to open their business."

Faulkner continued with his explanation, "You see Mack, currently the town people are in a defiant stage or denial stage. They don't want to admit that we're in charge. They are demonstrating to me that they want to fight this round the hard way. We have to break their spirit." During the later part of the late evening, mobs began to form. This time it wasn't just shop owners, it was some of McDowell's men. The moon was full and tension filled the air. The crowds grew bolder with every speech given by whomever could talk the loudest. The mob looked more like a lynch mob. Torches began to light up in the distant foreground. I said to Faulkner as he sat there playing a calm game of solitaire, "What a mixed up bunch of country backyard clod-hoppers. I think the crowd is on the way to break out McDowell." The crowd walked in front of the jail and stopped. I quickly loaded both of my shotguns.

The Captain got up and said, "Shit that was a winning hand. Mack, let me handle this situation." We walked out the office and I held my shotguns in the ready position. I stopped on the porch, but Captain Faulkner walked closer to the crowd. The crowd got silent.

The Captain recited something that was said by someone great. "Let the law be ruthless and order be restored, and let us make terror the order of the day. These words were spoken a long time ago." The Captain gave the crowd an angry cold look and continued, "Wonna make history today? Be my guest and try to liberate those assholes we got locked up. My men are itching for target practice today. If you look around, you'll notice that there are no guards to be seen. If you're inching for a fight or just want to be a part of history, I'm here to grant both wishes. Who's first?" There was a long pause. No one in the crowd flinched a muscle. The Captain continued, "I want all of ya'll to listen real good. Thirty innocent people were slaughtered one month ago. The law calls that murder, and murder is a hanging offense. You are all guilty of the murder of thirty innocent men, women, and children. You might not have pulled the triggers, but you know who did, and that makes you all accessories to a crime. Nobody is allowed to leave town until my investigation is complete. My snipers are located all around town for those who don't take my word seriously. Therefore, you are all under house arrest. As of right this moment, you are in violation of a Federally mandated curfew."

Captain Faulkner was interrupted by one of McDowell's men, "What gives you the right?"

Faulkner interrupted by pulling out his colt 45 and aiming it into the man's face, cocked the weapon simultaneously, and answering the interrupted question, "God all mighty, the President of the United States and this here loaded 45. By the way, you are under arrest for causing a disturbance. Is there any-one that has a problem, and wants to express their first amend-ment rights?" The Captain turned his back to the crowd. "Go ahead talk or shoot now, my back is turned." He waited for a moment and then turned around. "That's what I thought. There still might be hope for a few of you. What were you people think-ing about? Did you think for a moment that you would be exempt from retribution of the dead? Somebody has got to pay. I can't believe for one moment that you were going to break out that piece of shit that we got locked up. I know that all ya'll can't be that stupid."

As I listened to the Captain work the mob of people, it became apparent what Faulkner was trying to accomplish. He capitalized on a bad situation. He was successfully using reverse psychological warfare. He continued to work his new found audi-ence like a preacher on Sunday morning. I wondered if their attention was captured because of his viewpoint, or because they believed that our snipers had them targeted, or because the Captain had his weapon cocked and pointed his 45 at McDowell's man's head. In any case, he had control of the situation without firing a round. I was impressed by how he kept his composure. At last the Captain came to a peaceful conclusion, "This mob is an illegal assembly. Today is your lucky day, except for this soon to be locked up asshole," he said referring to McDowell's man. "I'm gonna allow you to go back to your loved ones unharmed. So, break this up and leave now! Except for you. Big mouth," he said. The gaggle broke up and dispersed quickly.

Early morning 8 July

It's interesting how hard times bring people together. Faulkner and I got to know each other in the short time that we were together. He was kind of a remote fellow and seldom opened up his thinking. I knew that he was very intelligent, but also a realist. I found out the best way to get him to open up was during a card game. I would never second guess him because of his rank, but also because I respected his judgment. Right after breakfast and after checking on the men, we had some time to kill. I had a lot of questions on my mind so I talked Faulkner into playing his favorite game of poker. As I was shuffling the cards, I opened up the dialogue.

"Sir that was a fine piece of work you did last night with that lynch-mob." I said.

Faulkner responded, "Thank you Mack."

"Sir, did you know that there were never any snipers targeting those people? They were all asleep. In fact most of our guys didn't even know that there was a disturbance last night." I dealt the cards. Faulkner looked at his hand, and laid three cards down on the table. I gave him three more cards. He smiled and answered, "Mack, like I've been preaching all along about this business of balance. Remember how I used the example about the pendulum? Well I felt that the pendulum began to move in the direction of McDowell last night when that lynch-mob approached us. I simply used an illusion to swing the pendulum back in our direction."

"I'm confused sir, please explain what illusion," I urged. "Remember early yesterday, our guards had been seen by everyone in town. Their presence was known because everybody could physically see them. Last night there were no guards to be seen. The illusion is what the mob didn't see. I merely used their imaginations against themselves. I used their own fear of the unknown as leverage to swing the pendulum back to our side." I simply grinned in disbelief, but was amazed with the Captain's ability to use his imagination. I looked at my hand and decided to discard two cards, and drew two cards. I had a three, four, and five of hearts. We used bullets as make believe money. A moment lapsed as we observed our cards. I asked the Captain, "Sir what's the next move?"

The Captain thought that I was referring to the card game. "Call Sergeant," Faulkner replied, while studying his hand.

"I was not referring to the card game. I meant what do we do now, here in this God forsaken town, with McDowell, and this crazy mission?" I asked.

The captain folded up his hand and leaned back in his chair in deep thought. "Well Mack, I'm not exactly sure. You know this is unknown territory that we jumped into feet first. I think we'll wait to get a response from the business community. Hopefully this curfew that we imposed will have an effect, however, it will take probably a few days for something to give." Faulkner refocused back to his card game. "I'll open the bet with five bullets."

I challenged the bet, "I'll see your five bullets and raise five more bullets."

Faulkner leaned back in his chair with a big smile, thinking that he had won this game and began taunting, "Now that's what I like, a sergeant with brass balls." I looked back at the Faulkner, wondering if he was bluffing. "Ok Mack, I'll match your five bullets, and call."

"Before I finish you off, I've got a few questions to ask you." I added, "Were you scared when you approached the crowd? Were you bluffing last night?"

Captain Faulkner started laughing and answered the second question first. "Mack, you might not believe this, but last night when I walked directly in the teeth of the crowd, I thought that you were behind me, and when I realized that you were not there I just about shit in my britches. Nevertheless, I was so pissed off at that loudmouth, I simply forgot about being scared. Was I bluffing? Maybe, or maybe not." Faulkner mood changed from a joking mood to a melancholy mood, "You know Mack, I was just thinking about what happened last night. I hope maybe some decent citizen will stand up for what's right. All we need is just one good citizen."

"What do you suppose happened to the sheriff?" I asked the Captain.

"I don't know," Faulkner answered.

"What about all of McDowell's men? They outnumber us 4 to 1?"

"I don't know."

"How long can we officially hold this town under curfew?"

"I don't know."

"Shit sir I'm glad that you got all the answers, I was beginning to get worried," I said sarcastically. I showed the Captain my hand. He looked in disbelief. "Shit, Mack, you lucky bastard. It looks like you've got all the answers."

Late night 8 July

The captain and I were playing gin rummy on the night of the eighth. We were playing gin rummy because Faulkner's poker skills stunk. At that point nothing had changed, and Faulkner lashed out in disappointment, "Damnit Sergeant! You lucky bastard."

I started taunting Faulkner, "How about a game of old maid? Damn sir, maybe I need to go across the street to the five and dime store and purchase a pair of jacks. You know what I was thinking?" I asked Faulkner.

Faulkner answered rather angrily, "I have no damn idea what you're thinking Sergeant. But I'm sure that you're gonna enlighten me with your effulgence."

I answered, "no I don't smoke." The Captain looked at me with a mystified look. He quickly realized that I had no idea what the word "effulgence" meant. Faulkner laughed at my eighth grade vocabulary.

"We haven't heard from McDowell's men yet." I went on, "Also why hasn't McDowell been more vocal?"

Captain Faulkner answered once again, "I don't know." At that time, there was a knock on the door. It was the town courier. For the past couple of nights we had been receiving notes from anonymous citizens. Most of the notes addressed McDowell's illegal activity, however, nobody was willing as of yet to come out of the closet. Faulkner's plan was working, but the development was slow.

Earlier in the day the Captain allowed the business owners to open up for business as a form of positive reinforcement. This allowed a better relationship between the Captain's men and a few of the business owners, although many of the townspeople remained skeptical. That night I decided to check on the Observation Point down the street from the Winking Lizard Saloon. As I approached the front door of the bell tower, heavily armed man walked out of the shadows and moved in my direction. The darkness enable me to see his face. His movement was absolute and methodical. His body language told me to be prepared for a fight. As I continued to close the distance I looked around the surrounding areas for an ambush. I decided to give him the impression that I wasn't alarmed by his presence. At about 20 meters and closing, he stopped walking.

I heard him call out, "That's close enough, nigger boy." He didn't realize that he had already reached the point of no returned by jerking my chain. I decided to allow him to voice his last rights.

The gunman continued to speak, "Well what do we have here? I see a gun toting nigger boy. You don't look that tough without that shotgun. Now do you boy?" I played along and stayed quiet. I could tell that my quietness boosted his confidence. He still didn't get it. I had this son of a bitch right where I wanted him. "What's the matter boy? Do you have a yellow streak running down your black back? Do you know how to use those pistols nigger boy?" he teased.

At last, I decided that he had used the N word enough. I said to the gunman, "You're gonna find out right this minute what this boy knows, you stupid, ignorant, clodhopping redneck. You see, what you fail to understand is that you have violated our curfew. There'll be no trial. I won't even take the time to throw you in jail, because you're just a slimy piece of shit slug that crawled from beneath an outhouse. Hell, I can see that trail of slime behind you. You're not worth my time, and tonight you're gonna die, make no mistake about it. Hell, I'm just talking to a dead man. Your not worthy enough of manhood status, you are dead...you.... wretched..... slug." I ended my speech with cynical laughter.

The gunman got quiet. I couldn't see his eyes or face but I could sense his frustration in his inability to win the battle of words. I knew that he really didn't want to fight, but he had reached the point of no return. I decided to rub salt into his wound even more. I angrily said to him, "Hey boy, when you reach hell, you can ask the devil for forgiveness." There was a long pause. I waited for him to make the first move. He didn't budge. I instigated the fight by saying, "Make a move, punk. Lucifer is waiting on you down there." I saw his hand jerk. I reacted by drawing both 45s, and fired with deadly aim. Both rounds hit center mass of his head and heart. He was dead before he hit the ground. I walked closer to see his face and to confirm his demise. I searched for an ID. When I pushed his blood soaked jacket back, I noticed that he was wearing a badge. It was the sheriff. "Oh shit" were the only words that came to my mind. I could feel a trapdoor open in the floor of my stomach. I looked around to see if there were any witnesses, and I saw a few lights from surrounding houses turn on. I quickly picked up the corpse and draped it over my shoulder, and took him into the church. I notified Faulkner and told him how this mishap had developed. Once again he summed up the situation quickly. He deducted that it was a setup. Unfortunately for me, I had fallen into the trap.

0700 July 9th

The morning brought on new developments. Events unfolded and I wasn't sure who was in control. The fog of this mission was rolling in once again. From that point on, our unit was on a high state of alert. Faulkner and I no longer played card games. We looked through the windows of the jailhouse and saw small groups of Buford citizens talking and occasionally pointing in the direction of where the gunfight took place between the sheriff and me.

Meanwhile, McDowell came out of his shell. For two days McDowell hadn't spoken a word until that morning. McDowell's voice called out from the jail cell in the back. "Captain Faulkner, hey Captain Faulkner, I would like a moment of your time," he yelled. Faulkner and I walked back to the prisoners. It seemed that McDowell had found new life. The deputies that were locked up began to taunt me. "You gonna hang black boy, you shot the sheriff. Murder is a hanging offense. You're not even worthy of a trial. You gonna get the lynch mob, black boy," one deputy said. I squelched my anger towards the ignorant deputy, and yet the Captain and I were bewildered as to how they knew what had happened.

McDowell interrupted the moment of confusion. "I pose no threat to you and your sergeant. I would like to have a moment alone with you please," he said.

Faulkner played along with McDowell's request and took him back into a secluded jail cell next to the coffee pot. Dialogue started between Captain Faulkner and McDowell. McDowell seemed to be rather confident and cocky as though the situation were under his control. McDowell poured two cups of hot coffee and handed one to the Captain. He spoke in a composed manner. "Captain Faulkner, in my many years of being a professional I have to complement you on this operation. You totally caught me off guard. Believe me when I tell you this. I deeply understand what you're trying to do. However, things aren't always what they seem."

Faulkner looked at McDowell, raised one eyebrow in a questioning slant, and responded, "Yeah, tell it to the innocent people that you slaughtered a month ago."

There was a pause as McDowell repressed his anger at Faulkner's comment. McDowell continued to say, "Yes Captain you're right about that slaughter. I tried to warn those people. Our citizens of Buford fought for the south. They had always been disgruntled toward the colored community. They were like a festering sore. There's been no healing of wounds since the war. The white community was just waiting for an excuse to strike. One day a little white boy got killed. He was found in the vicinity of the black village. A lynch mob was formed. I tried to stop them, but there were too many of them. By the time I made my way out to the village, it was too late. So you see Captain, I personally had nothing to do with that situation. Even today that case remains open. If you don't believe me go and check my books that you got locked up in the courthouse. The only hard evidence that is known is that the local Indians might have been involved."

Faulkner knew that McDowell was lying, but continued to play along with McDowell's game. McDowell continued, "Obviously you're a very smart man. I respect what you're trying to accomplish. But regretfully, you've been misinformed. I can help you. It's apparent that I have my faults. I also have a bunch of incompetent fools that work for me. You're not going to stay in the Army forever. Someday you'll need a good job. I need a good man like you. I could triple your income. You just name the price my good man."

McDowell's intention had become transparent to Faulkner. Like a sponge that had reached its saturation point, Faulkner responded in order to get a true reading of what McDowell was trying to achieve. Faulkner asked, "What about my friend, Sergeant Mack?"

McDowell's alter ego immediately surfaced. His face began to turn red and purple, and the veins in his neck surfaced. He cuffed his hands into a fist, his nose flared, and his mouth became grossly contorted. He stuttered when he spoke, "That..ni..nigger ain't your fa..friend. Captain, all you got to do is to leave. I'll take care of the rest. That boy in there is a dead man. He shot the sheriff in cold blood, and justice will be served."

The roles had changed between the Captain and McDowell. Faulkner was gaining composure and McDowell was becoming hot and flustered.

Faulkner replied, "So let me recap of what you are really trying to say. Mr. McDowell, I ask for you to voice your guidance if I falter in my understanding. You will pay me a large sum of money if I just simply leave?" McDowell nodded his head to show his acknowledgment. Faulkner continued, "You'll promise to continue your investigation on those innocent victims that were slaughtered one month ago today?" McDowell shook his head in agreement once again. He began to calm down. The Captain continued, "The sheriff has got nothing to do with your anger at Mack. You really want Mack because you simply want to satisfy your need for vengeance. Relax, Mr. McDowell you can be totally honest with me." McDowell relaxed.

He sat back into his hard wooden chair and said, "Yes Captain Faulkner. It's that simple." McDowell played into the captain's hand. Faulkner continued, "What are you going to do about the witness that was there the night you raided that village?"

McDowell's mood turned defensive. "Witness, what witness?" he demanded.

Captain Faulkner continued, "You didn't kill everyone. I confiscated your ledgers and they showed violations of misappropriations and extortion within your city government." McDowell's eyes were bulging from his sockets from disbelief.

Faulkner continued, "You're a stinky filthy lying rat, and should be expunged from the face of this earth,.. you.. two bit pimp."

McDowell tried one last gasp, "Don't be a fool, Captain. You're willing to throw your life away for a nigger."

Captain Faulkner continued, but this time he voiced his opinion in anger. "What part do you not understand, you… slithering snake? That Sergeant is my friend, and I would rather die two deaths before I turn my back on him."

McDowell's mouth contorted with anger once again and he responded, "I'll piss on your sorry grave, you fool."

Faulkner smiled and said, "Good, I hope the roses grow when you do. Sergeant Mack, come and get this asshole, and pitch him back in jail with the other idiots." The momentum of events picked up at an alarming rate. The fog of this conflict between good and evil thickened by the minute.

I approached the Captain after locking up McDowell. "Sir did you learn anything from that fool?" I asked Faulkner. "Yes, I think he's a little pissed off at us," Faulkner answered.

"Well sir, a few things have developed during your conversation with McDowell. I've got good news and I've got bad news. I'll give you the bad news first. Larger pockets of people began to form. Our guards have been breaking up the small pockets, but the masses are increasing in size." Faulkner thought for a minute, "Okay, from this point on until further notice, put a pad lock on all of the saloons. These townspeoples' courage increases when their alcohol consumption increases." With a look of alarm, I told the Captain about an observation by one of our scouts, "OP12, you know, our Navaho scout reports that activity has increased out at the McDowell ranch. He reports that more gunmen have appeared. He believes that they are preparing for something big."

Faulkner didn't have a response for that development, but his eyes brightened. "What about the good news Mack?" he asked. I handed Faulkner an encrypted message. "The

Commanding General from Fort Pulaski sent a telegram message that states that he will be sending in company to relieve us within a couple of days." Faulkner's face glittered with joy.

Later that day, another encrypted message was dropped off at our Command Post. The message was for Faulkner's eyes only. Faulkner took 10 minutes to decrypt the message. I finally heard him yell out in disbelief, "Unbelievable! Damnit, I can't believe this shit." Faulkner handed me the message, and it stated, "Mission number 540 clandestine activity must be aborted by 11 July 1878. Signed Commander in Chief, Rutherford B. Hayes."

"What are you orders, boss? Do we just give this town back to McDowell? What the hell is going on up in Washington?" I asked Faulkner. Captain Faulkner took a deep breath. I could tell that whatever happened went much deeper than what was disclosed in the letter. Faulkner became quiet and despondent. I could tell that for once he had been defeated. I figured that I'd better jostle what information I could out of him.

"Sir there's no time to flounder in pity. The lives of the men that you command depend on it. So with all due respect, what the hell is going on?" I asked.

Faulkner looked me straight in the eyes. "Okay, Sergeant Mack, I'll try to give you the condensed version. I'll start from the beginning. This unit was formed back in the early 1870s after the war. It was formed in response to the reconstruction of the South. During that time there were many enemies of the government, both foreign and domestic. President Grant couldn't use the army as a strong arm to stop pockets of political anarchy that kept developing within our government. This unit started out like a secret police, but later developed into a guerrilla warfare unit. This unit's main mission became clandestine in nature, but this unit was unpopular to many congressmen. Many believed that it was too expensive to fund covert operations. I personally felt the sting of funding about a year ago. When we stopped getting replacements and equipment. We used to have over a 120 soldiers in this unit. The soldiers that are here on this mission represent the last, including you and I. We're becoming involuntarily extinct, like the buffalos that used to roam the Northwestern frontiers. This mission represents last mission. Basically it's all about money. This is one hell of a way to end a mission, isn't it? McDowell has won and there's nothing that can be done about it. Tonight, we'll get the men together for a meeting to determine what to do next."

Later in the evening, I made my rounds to our outpost to deliver the message about the meeting that would take place that night. While en route to my last post, which was in the vicinity of McDowell's ranch, I noticed that another rider was following me. I hid in the woods and waited for the rider to close on me. He stopped inside the woods when he saw my horse. I popped out from behind a tree with the sights of my 30.06 pointed at him. It was the operative. I lowered my weapon. He stayed mounted on his horse.

The operative started babbling, "I heard what happened between you and the sheriff. You must be pretty damn fast. The sheriff was known as being one of the fastest at the draw on this side of the Mississippi."

I arrogantly replied, "Apparently not fast enough."

The operative continued, "I thought that I'd better tell you about a couple of developments so you can tell your Captain. That book with all of McDowell's contacts in it is out at McDowell's place. There's no chance in hell to get to it because it is heavily guarded. Also, McDowell's assistant, Kenneth Merriweather, intercepted the message about your relief coming on the tenth of July from Fort Pulaski. He plans to take his men and ambush them before they can reach Buford. Tell your Captain to get the hell out of Dodge while he's alive. These guys aim to bring a world of hurt on you. Well, that's all the news that I got. Good luck." The operative rode out fast and disappeared into the horizon. As soon as I got back I told the Captain. I felt then that the mission was totally cluttered with deceit and deception from the highest levels of government. The mission was no longer a mission to capture and expose McDowell's illegal operations. I felt that if we stayed much longer, we would no longer be in control of the situation. I figured that the Captain felt the same. This mission turned into a mission of survival.

0200 early morning July 10th

Our defense posture had collapsed and the observation posts were unmanned. We met in the horses' corral. All 32 personnel met with Faulkner, which we knew would be our last gathering as a unit. The mood was rather somber. There were no smells of coffee and cigar smoke. There were no maps, concept sketches, or black and white pictures. There was just the smell of hay and horse shit.

The Captain started his presentation, "At midnight this mission will be officially terminated. I don't know how the rest of you feel, but I'm not willing to hand this town back over to McDowell. You guys know what McDowell is capable of doing. The decent thing that we could do for humanity is to properly hand over this town to our relief that will be here on the eleventh. There is one problem if you decide tonight to carry through with this last request. We would be disobeying the orders of our Commander and Chief. Bottom line gentlemen this is a court martial offense." Faulkner quit talking to allow his message to sink into everyone's thought processes. Faulkner continued, "I plan to stay to make sure it's done right even if it means my death. I'm asking for volunteers tonight."

Once again Faulkner allowed his message to sink in. Sergeant Wilburn said, "Sir, I don't get it. I thought you knew us better than that. You act like we want to live forever or something." Corporal Mango, a Navaho scout that never talked about anything to anybody, became vocal with new life and interrupted Wilburn. He said, "Why don't we just hang McDowell tonight, and kick the living shit out of McDowell's boys tomorrow?" New life came back in the face of Faulkner as he saw that his men would support him even if it meant their deaths.

"Sir, today or tomorrow is a good day to die," I said. I looked at the faces of the men around the room. I spoke for them. "Sir, look around the room. I've got nowhere to go. I'd rather die an honorable death fighting for what's right, instead of working in some cotton field. Corporal Mango would rather be here with you instead of dying a slow death on some rat-infested reservation. We all joined this unit with a couple of things in mind. Honor and pride are what we're here for. I believe that's worth fighting for. We were chosen because of our special talents. Therefore I believe that it's appropriate to demonstrate those talents to the people who doubt them. We are warriors, the Vikings of the past. The action is here and so are we. What are your orders sir?" I asked Faulkner.

Energized with new life Faulkner answered, "I figure for once we'll do things the easy way. The main emphasis will be on delivering Buford over to our relief, and this is how we're going to execute this mission. Mack will take ten of you with him as guides or forward security. Your purpose will be twofold. Your main purpose is to guide the aid in delivering the relief, but your secondary target will be McDowell's house. The purpose for achieving this secondary target is to get that book with all the incriminating evidence. This book will provide us added protection. This secondary target will be a target of opportunity, which means that this target will only become active if McDowell relaxes his defense posture. I believe that once his men recognizes that one third of our element have departed to bring in the relief column, McDowell's men will throw every available man at the town in order to regain control before our relief gets here, and if that happens Mack and his men will be free to raid his place."

I was concerned with Faulkner's plan because this meant that we would be violating one important rule of war as a consequence of separating our forces. I immediately raised my hand with a question. "Sir, you know their powers in numbers, and you know McDowell outnumbers us four to one."

The Captain replied, "Yes, but remember his men don't know what they are actually up against. I personally hope that they do attack."

I realized then what the Captain was trying to achieve. I grinned at the Captain, and replied with a slight chuckle, "Sir, you're brilliant, you... sly dog you. You're picking a fight, so we can get the book."

Faulkner replied between laughter, "Yes, and they'll get ambushed when they attack. We will have our cake and eat it too." Everyone in the room broke out in laughter. Captain Faulkner's plans would be set in motion the morning of the eleventh. However, all day on the tenth we did nothing but help prepare the defenses for Faulkner. He imposed a curfew of the town's businesses. At this point Captain Faulkner didn't care about annoying the civilians. He was actually protecting them from getting caught in the middle of all the gunfire that would take place.

Faulkner set up a very complex and highly elaborate plan of defense. We were closing in on the deadline to abort the mission, but it didn't matter because the fight was on, and the cognitive Captain was back in business. Some soldiers and I broke into Buford General Store and confiscated coffee and cigars while Faulkner scratched out a concept sketch on the ground. Within minutes, the briefing room was set up the way it used to be. We are back in business again.

With the smell of coffee and cigar smoke in the air, Faulkner started the briefing with his well mannered ways, "Gentlemen, this new operation is based on a few historical facts and assumptions.

First the facts: McDowell's ass is locked up in jail, and his men will risk their sorry lives to save him. Up to now they have been successful, because their bullying tactics have been unopposed. I'll assume that they'll be cocky and haphazard in trying to spring the rat out of jail. It's a fact that they outnumber us four to one. And, I'm sure that they know this fact also, so I assume that they will try to use this to their advantage. If they knew who they were fucking with they wouldn't attack. Therefore, gentlemen we definitely have the element of surprise on our hand. We're going to win this fight because of their stupidity and ignorance," Faulkner said. "This is my vision of how I believe we will fight. Initially all sniper positions will be manned. The remaining 14 guys will be in different fighting positions to create the deception that our unit is larger than they anticipated. As McDowell's men attack from the east, our initial sniper will infrequently engage targets on the far side of Mill's creek. We want to give McDowell's men the perception that we are poor marksmen. Hopefully this action will boost their confidence to move inside. The soldiers in the initial positions will offer little resistance to the oncoming charge to give them the impression that we're not capable of fighting against a superior force. Those same soldiers will quickly move back into the next fighting positions, and clearly give McDowell's picture that we're on the run. Once his main body is lured into our kill zone, we'll quickly pop out of our hiding positions and ambush them. There will be a lot of independent action. That means that our professional skills will be truly tested. Last thing, Sergeant Mack and his group will leave mid-afternoon just before dusk on the evening of the eleventh. Therefore, our defense must be in position prior to their departure."

Early Morning 11th of July

We definitely weren't going to win the hearts and minds of the citizens of Buford because we trashed a lot of property when we built the defense. It look like a plague of locusts strip the place. The town store shelves were emptied. We reinforced buildings by taking, lumber, nails, and anything that was needed from the town's hardware store. We used the high tower hotel room as sniper positions. We knocked out all the glass windows and reinforced them with lumber to make firing potholes. We didn't have sandbags so we used furniture and revetments. All the ammunition and guns that were in the gun store were depleted from its inventory. Bags of wheat and grain were stacked in the middle of the street to be used as roadblocks. We were like a bunch of barbarians that took whatever we needed. The Captain figured that the appropriation of the town's assets was the price tag that the citizens would have to pay for their defense. I'm sure the citizens that were caught in the middle wondering, "Who are the bad guys, and who's the good guys?"

Mid-Afternoon 1200

Faulkner and I walked through the streets looking at the development of the defense setup. I was truly exhilarated by the Captain's professional skills in engineering this defense.

However, I had one question that bothered me so I asked him, "This defense is set up for McDowell's men to attack from the east moving in a westerly direction. What happens if they try to attack our Northern and Southern flank?"

Faulkner replied, "Very good question Mack. McDowell's men will attack in area that offers the least resistance. So, I've issued special instructions to our snipers that in the event that they sight McDowell's men on the northern and southern flanks. They should shoot to kill anything that moves at maximum distance. As we speak, they are clearing fields of fire for those particular flanks.

We have to give the perception that our northern and southern flanks are our strong points. I expect that they will probe us to find a weakness. I'm sure they know conventional Army doctrine. However, they don't realize that we're not conventional. Once they see that our eastern flank is the weak point they will attack it. And when they take the bait, we've got them."

"My complements, sir. It would be an honor to stay and fight with you sir." I was implicating to Faulkner my displeasure for my mission to get the book had lesser importance. Faulkner picked up my signal of indignation. We stopped walking and the Captain grabbed me by my shoulder. He looked me straight in the eyes and said to me, with resolved passion, "Mack make no mistake about it. Your mission is more important than mine. The power of McDowell isn't his gunmen. This conspiracy that McDowell supports is much larger than McDowell himself. That book will expose McDowell's employers. Also, that book may help exonerate this unit from getting court-martial. That book is our ace in the whole."

Late afternoon 1900 hrs.

My group of men were prepared to move out on the quest for the book, but we had to achieve our first mission, and that was to find and assist the Relief Column movement into Buford. I figured that would be the easy mission. The idea was once we made contact with the relief column, five others and myself would ride out to rob McDowell's quarters. Once this mission was completed, I was suppose to linkup with Faulkner at a predetermined rally-point. Captain Faulkner came out to wish me luck. Our eyes converged, and our minds became one. His face was contorted with worry. "Good luck Mack. It's unfortunate isn't it."

"What's unfortunate sir?" I asked.

Faulkner replied, "Unfortunate that the events control us. We no longer are in control of the events. Whatever happens, destiny will have its way, for the good, or for the bad. It seems that we're just a bunch of pawns in this large game of chess."

I mounted my horse and replied, "Sir, if that's true, your defense represents the checking move, and my gaining the book represents the check mate move of this dangerous game. It's too late to worry now. The fight is here, and so are we. There isn't enough time to look back, and wonder if we are doing the right thing. Right or wrong is insignificant. The end results is all that matters."

Faulkner looked at me and smiled. He saluted me and said, "Sergeant Mack I do believe we have a date with destiny."

I replied, "Absolutely, I'll either met you at our rally point or I'll meet you in the afterlife, sir." We left thundering towards our unknown destinations. I didn't want to look back.

2100 hrs.

We thundered through the dense canopy of woods, leaving nothing but a trail of dust behind us. I was leading the charge, guiding to the area where we would intercept the Relief column.

After a half hour of riding, we came to a bridge. I halted to make a map check and sent my Navaho scouting buddy across to check the far side of the bridge. I looked at my map, and I realized that we were not far from Black Jack McDowell's spread. I tucked my map back into my pocket when I saw the thumbs up signal from the scout. Like ducks in a row, we crossed the bridge, and suddenly we heard a distant shot. I immediately looked over to the far side of the bridge and saw the scout horse dragging my scout friend's body through the brier patches. His foot was caught in the stirrup. Immediately, a hell storm of bullets started zinging in every direction.

I heard one of the men cry, "Ambush!"

I looked in every directions and saw muzzle flashes. There was nowhere to run. There was nowhere to hide. We were stuck on an exposed bridge. There was no space to maneuver. The bullets started raking pieces of flesh off the horses. My friend's bodies were being riddled with hot lead. I tried to move everyone forward but the horses were panicking and we were losing control.

One soldier dismounted and tried to fire back. I saw him take at least ten rounds. A few of us tried to make our way back to the other side, but the volley of steel increased even more from the near side. Only a handful of us avoided shots.

We began to return fire while still mounted. A bullet zinged passed my ear, and ripped off the bottom flap of flesh. Another chunk of flesh was ripped from my side. I could feel warm blood trickling down my shirt. Suddenly, my horse took a couple of rounds and cried out. My horse and I tumbled off the bridge and onto the hard surface creek bed.

2000 hrs. Dusk that night

Hours later I woke up dazed and confused. I must have been there for a while, because it was almost dusk. I was in terrible pain from the bullet that winged my side. My head was pounding from either the fall or the bullet that took off a piece of my ear. I heard no horses or moans from the wounded. The only noises that I heard were from crickets and the bullfrogs. I knew deep down inside that nobody had lived through this ambush. I wondered if I was still alive.

I had to know if any of my friends lived through this act of butchery. This was a brutal ambush. All of my friends' bodies were riddled with bullet holes. They were so mauled by the bullets that I couldn't identify who was who. I felt remorse thinking of their families. With every passing second, my alter ego, the beast crept into my soul. With every drip of blood that fell from the corpses of my friend's bodies, the thought of retribution fulfilled the wounds of pain within me. From that moment on, that hour, that minute, that second, I vowed to anoint my wrath upon the people that were responsible. Nothing mattered anymore, because I wasn't dead in a physical sense, but from this point on I was just an empty shell, left with a large void. Revenge was what I needed and revenge was what I vowed to get. Only blood and death would fill my void. McDowell and anyone that followed him would know that I'm the avenging angel of death.

2030 hrs. July 11th Back in the town of Buford

Back in town, Faulkner had no idea about the unfortunate fate of my patrol. Hours had passed and the Relief column was nowhere in sight. Everyone was in place, ready to defend. The balance of the pendulum was now in the favor of McDowell's men but Faulkner was unaware of that.

Meanwhile, Charley Babb had orchestrated McDowell's small army. Their intent was simple. Charley knew that the town was lightly defended, especially after ambushing my patrol. He'd attack with overwhelming manpower and simply outgun Faulkner's element.

At 2031 hours McDowell's henchmen started their campaign to liberate Black Jack McDowell.

The day of retribution for the Negro settlement was about to unfold, and I wasn't around to take part in the festivities. These henchmen were the same raiders that took part in that heinous crime a month ago today. At this point they had never tasted defeat, but Faulkner and his boys were ready and poised to except the challenge. McDowell and his henchmen stopped on the outskirts of the city limits to briefly scan the town. He was limited to see the distant town defense posture. The towns to them looked desolate and quiet. Unknown to them Sergeant Young was in a treetop sniper post and spotted McDowell's men that were observing the town. He relayed this information by hand signals to Sergeant Rogers who was located at the base of the courthouse.

He yelled to the soldiers that had gathered around the church bullshitting, "It's show time." Rogers then ran into the jail to notify the Captain.

McDowell heard the commotion. He jumped out of his bunk and ran to the jail bars and yelled to the Captain, "There's still time you fool."

While walking out the door, Faulkner stopped and turned around to issue his last order to Sergeant Wilhalm, who had the mission of watching the prisoners. Faulkner said to Wilhalm, "If those son of a bitches make it through our defense, scatter McDowell's brains all over the wall." The Captain quickly scrambled to the initial fighting position. The town was ready and properly prepared. The streets were littered with furniture and debris to act as gauntlets to slow down and break up large formations. The fighting positions were reinforced with lumber. The sniper positions were camouflaged and fully manned.

The massive formation of McDowell's men moved. Sniper position 1 fired at the formation as they approached Mill's Creek. Sniper position 2 fired as they crossed Mill's Creek. The Captain's plan was working. The inaccurate sniper fire deceived McDowell's men. They took the bait, so their approach would be from the east. The unyielding mass of men made their way to the edge of the wood-line and the open terrain that lead into town. With the massive amount of dust, debris, and gunfire, Faulkner and his men on the ground had difficulty in acquiring a clear target. Faulkner quickly moved his ground team back to the next fighting position, because he knew that it would be difficult to break the raiders' momentum.

The snipers had a clear view of their targets. To them it was a turkey shot. The gunfire was random. Resistance appeared to be light. Every shot that they took meant death to one of McDowell's men. Each sniper shot at a different time, causing confusion. McDowell's men could not focus on one particular sniper. Suddenly, the mass formation of mounted men ran into the gauntlet of roadblocks in the streets. The violent speed of McDowell's momentum carried them crashing into the gauntlet. Horses tumbled over furniture, hurling riders through the air, and inflicted mortal wounds. Faulkner's snipers continued to do their deadly jobs of accurately taking out the target, to include the riders that were hurled off their horses. To make matters worse McDowell's men were being trumped over by the second and third ranks of riders. The second ranks of rider tried to dismount, but then their momentum brought them into Faulkner's killzone. "Give it to them, boys," he cried out from behind their hide position, triggering his ground force to open fire. McDowell's second element of men were in total bafflement from Faulkner's ground ambush and snipers. To make matters worse, McDowell's third and final echelon of men galloped up the middle of the mayhem. They were trapped inside the confines of Faulkner's web of death. Everything caught in the vice of the kill zone was being slaughtered. Men and horses cried out as they tumbled to their deaths. The momentum of the attack reversed into a futile attempt to fight back. Still, everywhere McDowell's men turned, deadly crossfire inflicted fatal results. Panic had begun to enter the defeated minds of McDowell's men. They tried to backtrack their way out of the kill zone, but they they kept tumbling over the dead men and horses that littered the streets. The only option left for McDowell's depleted few was to run for their lives. That option no longer remained opened, because Faulkner's snipers cut off their pursuit. The once organized formation of raiders was now isolated into a disorganized gaggle. Within minutes, Faulkner's ground crew mopped up the futile resistance.

When the gun-smoke cleared, dead men and horses stretched a mile from Mill's Creek up to the bank of Buford. Forty-two of McDowell's fifty-one men were killed or wounded by the ambush.

Faulkner and his men roamed the cluttered streets. Streams of blood ran from the corpses of the dead, which reminded him of his past battles that he fought during the Civil war. He was disgusted with the destruction, he felt vindicated for the pain and suffering that these same men had inflicted on the innocent.

Faulkner had his men line the dead, in a straight line in the street, for identification purposes. He wanted to see how much damage he had inflicted on McDowell's command structure. After walking through the dead bodies, Faulkner found Charley Babbs' corpse. Somehow, Cecil Radford, Kenneth Merriweather, and Henry Ambrose were nowhere in sight.

Faulkner decided to rub salt into McDowell's wound. Faulkner had Sergeant Wilhalm bring Black Jack out to see what was left of his small army. Wilhalm propelled McDowell's frail body out the doors of the sheriff's office onto the dusty streets. Immediately McDowell eye's were transfixed by the carnage before him. Faulkner grabbed McDowell by the collar, enraged by the sight of McDowell's existence. The Captain hurled McDowell body down to the ground, next to Charley Babbs' corpse. Faulkner pulled out his pistol, aimed it at McDowell's head and said, "I'm the judge, jury, defender and prosecutor. Court is now in session. You are responsible for crimes committed against humanity, God, your country and me. How do you plead?" McDowell just lay on the ground sweating profusely, eyes glazed with horror. Captain Faulkner continued, while his men watched the spectacle.

"Guilty as charged, you yellow belly piece of shit." He locked the hammer back on his pistol. Faulkner paused to allow McDowell to think about all the wrong that he committed in his life. Faulkner continued to taunt McDowell, "Praying ain't gonna do you any good, because God isn't listening." Another long pause allowed McDowell to consider his wrongdoing. McDowell's skin had turned pure clammy white.

Finally, Faulkner started to laugh and re-holstered his pistol. He yelled out to the Sergeant, "Wilhalm come and get this slug and throw his ass back in jail."

2100 July 11th

The aftermath of the battle brought an eerie quietness upon the town of Buford. It felt like the calm before the storm. Was the fight over? What ever happened to Cecil, Kenneth, and Henry? Faulkner's defense worked to perfection. However, he wondered about me and the Relief Column's absence. In addition, they had overextended their stay in Buford. He didn't have the manpower to send out another scouting party. Therefore, the only option Faulkner had was to wait for the relief column.

I lucked out and found my horse. He was wandering around, probably confused like me. I was glad to see him because he was the only thing that had survived that ambush. I was still dazed from the fall. My mind was scattered into many thoughts. I stopped for a moment and sat beneath an old oak tree to gather my thoughts. It was a peaceful night. The night sky glistened with stars. The full moon projected our shadows. There was a slight breeze that drifted in from the Atlantic.

Finally my thoughts were becoming one. I thought about the mission. I felt optimistic that the relief column should have linked up with Captain Faulkner by now. I had hope that they had better luck than I did. I figured that surely by then Faulkner should be on the way back home again. It would be a dishonor for me to go back. I failed to find the column and had failed to get the book. The feeling of revenge detonated inside my guts. I could clearly see the faces of the men that I left dead on the bridge. There was only one out for me. I mounted my horse. I had to get that book, by whatever means.

An hour later, I navigated in the black of night to McDowell's spread. His property was aligned with barbwire fence. I could see

McDowell's cattle wandering around grazing on the grass. They were probably stolen, and the beef was probably used to feed his small army. I walked and observed the vast white puffy cotton fields that were used to fund McDowell's reign of exploiting the weak. I initially suspected that I'd run into one or two of McDowell's men lurking around. At this point I didn't care who saw me. I wouldn't be denied of the opportunity for my day of redemption. I got lost in my fury to cleanse McDowell's scum off the face of the earth. I lost track of time. Somehow I found myself outside the entrance of McDowell's mansion. Either everyone was asleep or dead, because I casually walked my way up to the porch without being spotted. I was outside of myself. I felt that I had nothing to live for. In any case death is the only sure thing in life, and if I bit the bullet today, so be it.

I was fully armed to deal death. I wasn't gonna leave that mansion without that book. In my left hand I carried a sawed off double barrel shotgun, and in my right had I carried my 30.06 shotgun. I was packing two 44 caliber colt six shooters on my hips, and two 38 caliber on my shoulder holsters. My pockets were full of shotgun shell, and my pistol belts were full of bullets. My attitude was right. Killing was the order of business. Kill first, get the book second, was the priority of business.

I locked the shotgun hammers to the rear and approached the door. Lucky for me, McDowell's men left the door cracked to catch the cool breeze of the night. Unknown to them they were going to catch hot pellets of my shotguns.

I bolted through the door and unloaded my sawed off double barreled shotgun in the direction of two of the three men that were playing a card game, partially splattering their insides on the floor. The other was so paralyzed with horror he didn't have time to react as I blew his head off with my 30.06 rifle. Quickly, I reached into my pocket, grabbed two rounds, broke my double barrel shotgun down, reloaded, and locked the hammers back.

Another gunman appeared out of his bedroom, dressed in gray long-johns. I instantaneously blasted him back into his room with my 30.06 shotgun. Blood sprayed in every direction. Already within a few seconds of entering McDowell's mansion, four of his gunmen lay dead. As I walked through the blood soaked floor down the hall towards the bedroom, a distant gunman leaped from behind the staircase, firing inaccurately with six-shooters in my direction. His bullets zipped past my head, hitting and breaking a glass fixture behind me. I fired both shotguns in his direction, which grotesquely mangled his body into hunks of bloody flesh. Like a shark smells the sent of fresh meat, I heard a door from the upstairs closing, which lured me towards that direction. At this point I was totally obsessed with vengeance. While walking in that direction I reloaded my tools of death. When I got to the door, I didn't bother kicking it in. I blasted the door with my double barrel, splattering wood-chips, glass and other debris in all directions. I bolted in to look for my next target, however, he was spared my vengeance. The combination of my shotgun pellets and wood splinters had accidentally, but mercifully put him to his death. Either McDowell's men were all dead or they were too chickenshit to screw with me, but I found myself alone in what looked like McDowell's library. I looked down at the corpse that was lying in his puddle of blood, face first to the floor. In his hand was a small leather binder. I couldn't believe my eyes. It was the book that I had come for. I guess I had caught him as he was trying to get rid of its contents. Just as I grabbed the blood soaked book I heard the pattering of feet shuffling out of the door. Once again, my alter ego took control of me. I looked out of the widow of the library and saw four men trying to escape with their lives. Without delay, I broke the window glass with the butt of my 30.06, and threw down my double barrel shotgun. The gunman that had just cleared the porch took a shot at me. Abruptly, I returned fire, inflicting a mortal wound through his chest cavity. I cut the others down in succession. The killing portion was over. Nevertheless, I wanted to send a message to all the people who supported McDowell's evil corrupted ways of living. In cold blood, I shot all of his livestock. I didn't even spare a chicken. I burned down his barns and horse corral and I set his lovely cotton fields on fire. I spared his mansion because I wanted everyone to see the carnage. I wanted everyone to know that McDowell's diary had been confiscated. It was approaching dusk and I had to leave. I had to be at least 4:00 o'clock in the morning. My plan was to use the swamps as my escape route to link up with Faulkner and my friends. I figured nobody would be able to pick up trail through the swamps of Buford, South Carolina.

7:00 O'clock Early Morning July 12 Back in the Town of Buford

Two days had passed since the deadline for aborting the mission. The relief column was one day late. Captain Faulkner knew that his unit could no longer hold the town of Buford under restriction. McDowell and his hoodlums were a justifiable fight. The citizens of Buford were on the brink of open rebellion. Before the conflict with McDowell's men, the citizens' patriotism had begun to sway in the direction of Faulkner's men. However, their minds had changed after the Captain imposed his will upon the business community property to fight the defense and the police state curfew didn't help relations either. At about 0730, an observation post located two miles east on the far side of Mill's Creek, relayed a message was sent by a mirror reflection. The message was relayed to OP 2, which was located on top of the town's water tower.

The message read, "VIP with at least 100 men heading in our direction, and will arrive within twenty minutes." The message was then relayed to Faulkner. He knew that VIP meant General Officer. He was astonished that a General Officer would be riding with a relief column. What ever the case, Faulkner assumed that the remainder of the mission would be handed over to the General. He had always believed that someone of higher rank should have handled this delicate mission. He also knew that a diplomatic solution would have to be worked out with the locals. Faulkner's priorities changed from this sensitive mission to getting his men back home safely. Euphoria had begun to settle on Faulkner's unit as they began to see the dust clouds kicked up by the column of Cavalry soldiers.

Sergeant Wilhalm looked at the Captain after noticing the approaching relief column and said, "Sir, it looks like we might live through this shit after all." Good cheer radiated throughout Captain Faulkner's ranks. All of his men gathered their gear and prepared themselves to move out. The observation points became inactive and his men moved in to show their respect for the General. The large body of Cavalry soldiers galloped through the streets in company column. They looked as if they were on parade. The large bodies of men stretched from one end of the street to the other. The column came to a halt when it reached the jail. Faulkner and his men were standing at attention lined up along the sidewalk in front of the sheriff's office. The Captain was center mass of the formation. It was easy to spot the General because he was overdressed. He was a tall, obese man, with an overflowing belt line, blue eyes, and wore a long nestling beard.

"Sir, my complements to the General," Faulkner reported. He held his salute for a moment. There was a short pause as the General looked around at the thunderstruck town. He returned the Captain's salute.

"Captain Faulkner, I presume. ...My name is Brigadier General George Renalds the III. My orders are to take over this Operation. Let me have your weapon, my good Captain." the General demanded. Faulkner gave the General a long searching look. He acted as if he didn't hear that request.

"Sir, could you repeat that question?" Faulkner asked. The General repeated,

"Captain, let me have your revolver." Faulkner reluctantly gave the General his weapon.

"Captain, are all your men present?" the general asked. Another long pause ensued as Faulkner evaluated the situation. Faulkner assumed that he was being court martialed for disobeying the order to abort this mission two days earlier. Faulkner's men had no idea what was happening.

"Most of them are here," Faulkner answered. "Sir, what is this all about?" the Captain asked the General. Without warning, the Captain saw a disturbing sight. Cecil Merriweather and Henry Ambrose McDowell's right hand men came galloping to the front of the Company Column of US Cavalrymen. Faulkner's eyes never left the two hoodlum's arrival.

The General rudely pushed Faulkner aside and answered his question, "You and your unit are gonna find out. I have an announcement," the General yelled loudly. "This unit is under arrest. Each individual will be court-martialed on the charges of treason."

There was a long silent pause. Immediately the Captain knew that he and his unit had been doubled crossed, but he also knew that his men would never be taken alive either. In fact, Sergeant Wilhalm, who was watching McDowell, overheard the conversation. He had already placed the crosshairs of his Remington rifle scope at the General's heart.

The General gave Faulkner a scorching look and continued his demands, "Captain have your men drop their weapons, and release Mr. McDowell." Faulkner had confirmed in his mind that there had been a conspiracy, but this time they were caught at a disadvantage. A dangerous poker game of death had begun between Captain Faulkner and General Reynolds.

The general started getting annoyed with Faulkner's slow

methodical stalling tactics. "We can do this thing the hard way or the easy way," The general threatened.

Faulkner replied with a defiant grin, "Sir, my men already know that the highest criminal charge that we could be charged with is insubordination, under the articles of Uniform Code of Military Justice." "If that's so Captain you are now in violation of your first general order. And in my book, that's treason," the General replied.

Faulkner composed his answer in the war of words. "Sir, it's apparent that you don't even know the first general order, you fuckin fat piece of shit." At that point, the general was obsessed with anger. He yelled out to the company commander of the relief column. The Column Commander Captain Yeager, a thinly built Captain, was charged to escort the General to Buford. He and his men weren't aware that they were there to arrest Faulkner, on the same hand Faulkner didn't understand Yeager's situation either, because Yeager's men were still mounted, and casually observing the spectacle. Faulkner decided to use Yeager's ignorance as leverage. The General had become obsessed with Faulkner's insubordinate action and screamed at Yeager, "Captain Yeager, have your men dismount and arrest this man and his men for treason,… Now!"

Faulkner didn't outright challenge. He calmly responded, "Captain Yeager, before you do that, does it make sense for a Brigadier General to be conducting a mission like this?"

The General was in a total rage because of Yeager's hesitation. "Damnit Captain Yeager, they are illegally holding the judge, mayor, and deputies of Buford hostage in that jailhouse." Faulkner could sense that the General was losing credibility because of his behavior. The General grabbed Captain Yeager by the shoulder and began to push Yeager towards the sheriff's office, yelling at the top of his lungs. "Let's go in the office I'll prove it to you, and then I'm gonna court martial you for disobeying a direct order. Come on you idiot," he yelled.

Faulkner stopped the General in his tracks. "Sir, there is a rifle pointed directly at your heart. If you take one more step towards that jailhouse there won't be a place on your chest large enough to pin any medals." Captain Yeager was caught between a rock and a hard spot, so he hesitated and did nothing. Everyone involved was in a state of confusion. The General had turned into a deranged madman. He pulled out Captain Faulkner's confiscated pistol from under his belt and shot Faulkner twice in the chest. Faulkner's body plunged to the ground. Faulkner's men watched in horror. Captain Yeager and his men watched in confusion.

The impulsive General felt vindicated for his actions. Sergeant Wilhalm focused the crosshair of his Remington rifle on the General and pulled the trigger, blasting a small hole through his chest and leaving a gapping hole in his back. Everyone was paralyzed with the shock of events.

Cecil Marriweather slithered his way towards the sheriff's office. He quickly took out his 45 and shot through the window of the sheriff's office, killing Sergeant Wilhalm.

Then the explosive power keg of events blew up. Faulkner's men fired and killed Cecil. Captain Yeager panicked and fired and hit one of Faulkner's men. Faulkner's men returned the favor, killing the Captain. The two groups of men exchanged gunfire. Faulkner's men were all killed after the heavy exchanges of up close fighting. It was simple mathematics: 18 men against 100. Faulkner's entire unit was dead except for me. They'd been extinguished, like the buffalo that wondered the northern plains. Was the mission a success?

CHAPTER 10

AFTERMATH

JULY 12 1878 DUSK: BACK AT MACK'S POSITION.
LOCATION: BEYOND THE SWAMPS
(Continuation from Chapter I. 2000 hrs)

I woke up from a deep sleep and mused over how I had gotten here. It was time to think about where I needed to go. I studied the soaked map once again to figure out what route to take to meet Captain Faulkner and the rest of the men. After considering how much time I had lost in the swamps, I decided to take a calculated risk and cruise my way through the cattle-trading town of Deadwood. The town ran parallel with Buford. After all, it would save me a half a day's ride. I allowed my gear to dry out, got a couple hours of rest. I jumped on my horse and started my journey toward the linkup point.

It was a hard night's ride. I didn't worry about McDowell's men anymore, because it didn't matter to me if they found me. My soul was adrift, floating in the confines of total retribution. I no longer could deny that I was in control of my own destiny. Destiny controlled me.

At the same time that I was approaching the outskirts of Deadwood, the night sky blackened with clouds. A rolling wind blew in from the east hurling thick sheets of rain against the ground. I figured this would be the best opportunity to stroll my way through Deadwood without being noticed. I approached the main street that lead into town. Between the splattering of raindrops on the ground and my horse galloping through the streets,

I could hear the distant sound of music coming from the direction of the town's saloon. Other than the rain and the music, the streets were quiet. I looked for a stall to water my horse, and once again my keen sixth sense picked up trouble moving in my direction. I wasn't sure if it was a case of fate or just bad luck.

Out of the night horizons, a group of eight to ten horsemen were approaching me from the opposite direction. My guts had begun to tighten. I wondered if it was a posse of lawmen, McDowell's men or just some riders of the night. It was too early to tell. They didn't make any sudden moves, therefore I did the same. As they approached, I could sense that they were McDowell's men. I wasn't going to run, because that meant going back through the swamps. If I stayed with my course, they'd identify my dark blue uniform, and the skin tone. The continuous downpour of rain kept their attention. My destiny with death made the choice for me. My mind kicked into gear about how I was going to fight this battle, because it was inevitable what was going to happen next. I quickly looked around at the surrounding buildings. The buildings were too close together to hide and duck into an alley. I glanced at the distant mob. They had closed at least 100 yards. Adrenaline started to pulsate throughout my body. They were approaching me from the left side of the narrow street. I slowly stopped my horse and dismounted on the right. I loosened up the straps that attached my double-barreled shotgun. I pulled off the leather safety straps that were attached to my 45s. The mob was closing their distance and they hadn't identified me. My plan was simple. The plan was to allow the riders to get within point blank range and blast my way through them. Hopefully my edge would come from the shock of my shotguns. Chaos, confusion and the percussion of my shotguns should do the job. As they closed within fifty yards, my anxiety level increased. My beastly alter ego was taking over once again. Was it rage, insanity, or just self survival? I don't know, but whatever it was, it took over my actions.

The riders were now within close shotgun range. They didn't notice my actions until I pulled out both shotguns. The closest rider's eyes focused in my direction just as I aimed and blasted them off their horses. The sound of the blast sent the horses and riders into a total state of pandemonium. I dropped my double barrel to the ground and used my 30.06 pump, blasting with total reckless abandon into the crowd. Three more riders fell off their horses dead before they hit the ground. Nonetheless, by now a couple of the mob had drawn their pistols, but their unsettled horses wouldn't allow them to accurately engage me. In haste, I drew my 45s, blasting another rider off his horse. The other two riders took off in haste when they saw that my will to fight couldn't be broken. Men and horses lay dead in the middle of street in the town of Deadwood. I gathered the corpses' weapons and bolted out of town towards my linkup point.

11:30 PM in the town of Deadwood 30 minutes after Mack's encounter with McDowell's men.
Continuation of Chapter II (Marshall Carr's point of View)

Marshall Carr returned from his murder investigation that took place on the McDowell's ranch. He was mystified of the destruction that took place there. He had planned to go back to his office in Deadwood to file a report on his finding, and then go home and get a well-deserved rest. However, as his two deputies, the doctor, and the marshall approached the entrance of Deadwood, crowds of citizens had gathered around the repugnant sight. The marshall was dumbfounded by this act. Moments later the the doctor examined the dead men wounds, he confirmed Marshall Carr's belief. The same types of weapons caused the wounds at the McDowell's ranch and in his town. All were done at close range. Once again, there were no witnesses. To make matters worse, footprints were covered up by the rain and mud. The marshall felt compelled to do something since he was the territorial marshall, but he was not fool enough to go chasing after that nightmare. He knew that he'd need outside help.

0600 13 JULY AT THE LINKUP POINT WHERE SERGEANT MACK WAS SUPPOSED TO LINK UP WITH CAPTAIN FAULKNER.

I made it to the linkup point a few minutes before dusk. The linkup point was three miles south of the border of Georgia and South Carolina. We were to meet in at a small deserted mineshaft. I sat down under a tree thinking about how I had blasted my way through those men. Once again I was totally out of control. It seemed to me that I was outside myself. This rage of anger could no longer be manually turned off. This fury couldn't be stopped, but for now, I was able to contain it.

Finally after a couple of hours, a sight for sore eyes came riding over the horizon. It was my friend Corporal Fitzpatrick. My initial thought was that he was riding as scout for the main body and Captain Faulkner. Moments later, Fitzpatrick told me the disturbing news. We stayed at the linkup sight for hours exchanging information. Fitzpatrick brought me up to date on the shocking events. Fitzpatrick picked up his story during the gunfire exchange between the Cavalry Company and our unit.

"At the time I was located on the furthermost outpost. When the gunfight erupted, I quickly moved up on the ridge that overlooked the town and used my binos to see what was going on. All of our friends had been massacred. Moments later, McDowell had been freed. Faulkner's body had been dragged into the sheriff's office and all the remaining bodies were dragged away. Hours later, the citizens started back to rebuilding Buford. I think they covered everything up that they could. Wanted posters were posted throughout the town with your name and description. You're wanted for the murder of the sheriff of Buford, the murder of the General, assaulting a government official, barn burning, and horse theft. McDowell himself put a large bounty on your head. McDowell no longer has a large army. He no longer has a strangle hold on the town of Buford, from what I gathered. Oh yeah, by the way, I believed that operative must have sold his services to McDowell, because he appeared after our friends had been slaughtered."

Fitzpatrick had helped me put the pieces of the puzzle together. It all became clear to me now. I opened up McDowell's diary, suspecting to confirm my belief on the involvement of the general. On the second page of the diary was the general's name. I began to summarize for Fitzpatrick the Government involvement. "What happened is when Washington sent that wiring telegram to us, somehow the general intercepted the message. The general reacted in fear of becoming exposed and connected with illegal activities in Buford. He knew the day that we were suppose to abort this mission, which was on the eleventh of July. He wanted to move in with the relief column on the twelfth of July. That would feloniously incriminate our unit on charges of subordination. Unfortunate for us, this case will be closed because there are no known witnesses, except for me, and now I'm considered a felon. Except for you, Fitzpatrick. You're the last of the living, Corporal. Nobody knows of your existence." I thumbed through the diary and stopped midway through my examinations of the listed names. With a quivering voice and pensive look I said to the Corporal, "You cannot go back home. There's probably nothing left standing at our home base. This name that's in McDowell's diary is the same name that signed the aborting orders. McDowell has got contacts in Washington."

Both of our eyes were haunted with inner pain. We had no future, no hope, and nowhere to go. I began to feel complete again when an idea surfaced. I explained to Fitzpatrick, "We've got one shot. It's a long shot but, but it's the only one that we'll get." I quickly copied the names of as many of the culprits out of the book on the map. I gave the corporal the book. "Get this book to retired Sergeant McCish. Explain to him what happened and he'll know what to do. So leave this place now. You have a better chance in getting back through than I do." Fitzpatrick mounted his horse and looked at me with concerned. I think he knew deep down what I was planning to do.

"Your going back to Buford aren't you?" Fitzpatrick asked me. I didn't answer. "They'll kill you dead, Sergeant Mack."

I replied, "I'm already dead, Corporal."

Fitzpatrick shouted with anger, "Don't you get it Sergeant Mack? This mission is over."

I shouted back at Fitzpatrick, "No, Corporal. I beg to differ. The mission might be over, but the job isn't completed. You, McCish, or the President of the United States can't save me. However, you have a chance to vindicate all of the dead, and help their families. Meanwhile, I appoint myself the angel of vengeance for our dead. So you must understand that I no longer control my destiny. Destiny controls me." I calmed down and lowered my voice one octave, "You must go now to do the most important thing. Forget me I'll be fine. Just go,… and good luck." Fitzpatrick saluted me and bolted out on his quest.

15th of July Marshall Carr Investigation Leads him to Buford
(Marshall Carr point of view)

I walked around, looking at all the bullet holes in various establishments. I knew that whatever happened here was bigger than a small scrimmage. I tried to make a connection between the big brawl that took place there, at McDowell's ranch, and my town of Deadwood. I drew the path of events that happened between the time I was notified about the disturbance at McDowell's ranch on the eleventh of July. I remembered that I didn't return to Deadwood until 11:30 the night of the eleventh because we spent most of our time hunting for a ghost. So whoever or whatever hit this town, did it when I was out investigating.

So far, the only victims killed were all McDowell's men. I couldn't figure out what the motive was. I tried to interview some of the citizens, but they were all tight lipped. It wasn't a secret to me that McDowell employed most of the shop owners. I should have known that they wouldn't speak against their own boss. I was told that a black man that escaped had killed the sheriff. How could a gang of men ride into town, shoot up the town, and escape unharmed? Where were all of the dead? It became clear to me that whatever preempted this chain of killing happened much earlier than twelfth July. I tried to interview McDowell. He became rude and belligerent. I could see that I wasn't going to gain any ground. In fact, he threatened my job, and then he ended his conversation with, "Marshall, get the fuck out of my town." I took his advice and left. I deducted that someone had finally pushed McDowell back, with reasonable success. I believed that they are not finished pushing. McDowell had cleverly covered up his tracks, because I wasn't able to get any hard evidence on the situation. This Mack guy who was wanted for shooting the sheriff must have done something to trigger rage and vengeance. In any case, I concluded this investigation for now. The only course I had left was to be patient and wait for something to happen, because I was sure it wasn't over yet.

9 MONTHS LATER MARCH 10TH 1879 BRUNISWICK, GEORGIA
MACK HAS BEEN IN HIDING. HE WORKS IN THE BRUNISWICK SHIPPING YARDS AS A LABORER.

The smell of fish was getting to me. I could no longer take this stench. It was time to blow this joint, because it had served its purpose. This job provided me with necessary cover to evade bounty hunters, the law, and the Army. The itch for revenge had become a part of my everyday thinking, and yet I had to allow McDowell to lower his guard. I was going back to Buford to set the record straight.

The first son of a bitch that I was going to get was the operative. That bastard sold his allegiance to McDowell. I figured the punishment had to fit the crime. My plan was simple. The plan was to infiltrate the town, observe my victim's daily habits for a couple of days, and strike hard and deep. I wanted McDowell, but the operative was my first priority, because he was the one that broke the faith. His act was a direct insult to the honor of our dead.

Once again I was on the move, but this time I was well rested and had money that I saved during my employment at the shipping yard. I traveled at night and slept during the day. My route took me back through the town of Deadwood. Luckily, this time there was nobody in the streets when I passed through. I made my temporary home on the outskirts of Buford. I constructed several observation points from different places around the ridges of Buford. That way I could get different vantage points to give me better angles of my target. I could clearly see most of the activity that took place in the streets of Buford. On the fourteenth of March I observed activity from dusk to dawn, nonetheless, that morning I saw McDowell coming out of the hotel. He was en-route to work. I assumed that he must live in town, because I had burned his place to the ground. Another observation that I made was that the mood of the people was totally different. When McDowell walked through the streets, most people greeted him with a smile. McDowell even stopped to greet old ladies and have lengthy conversation with shop owners. Either McDowell's henchmen were all dead or in hiding because I didn't see any of them.

Later that night I saw my target, the operative. He seemed to be one of those guys that lived in the fast track. He'd scampered from bar to bar. After one night of drinking he'd stagger his way back to the hotel where he was staying. I guess I could have moved in for the kill immediately, but time was on my side. I wanted to make sure that there would be no surprises.

Early morning March fifteenth I moved to a different outpost that over looked the town from the rear. It was about 0500 hours and all was quiet in the streets of Buford. Like the days before everything fell into place once again. Later that evening, the gathering of citizens formed in front of courthouse. Citizens came from all directions for this gathering. Store owners closed shops, the bank closed, and anybody that was somebody came to the gathering. My target made an appearance. The mood of the mass was jovial. The mayor walked out of the courthouse to talked to the crowd. When he walked out, the crowd acknowledged his presence by clapping and cheering. I listened in on his announcement.

"I have two introductions to make. The first introductions is Buford's new sheriff," he said. The courthouse doors opened and Henry Ambrose walked out. He was wearing a sheriff's badge. I was overwhelmed with this new development. I remembered that this guy was one of the original targets before our mission was aborted. After Ambrose gave his two minute speech, the mayor came back out to introduce his next guest. "Ladies and gentlemen, I want to introduce to you the leading candidate for the Governor of South Carolina. He is the city's number one citizen. I will now introduce you to your next Governor, Judge McDowell." McDowell walked out, all smiles and cheer. I was totally dumbfounded by the announcement. From that point on, I knew that McDowell was untouchable. If I took him out, it would be considered an assassination. An assassination would have a devastating effect on the innocent blacks that dwelled in South Carolina.

I refocused my attention on my target, the operative. With all these new developments unfolding, I assumed that Ambrose would probably appoint the operative as one of his deputies soon. Therefore, I felt compelled to get the job over quickly. I intended to do the job the following night once I confirmed the operative's nightly moves once more.

Late that night the operative made his normal appearance at the Winking Lizzard Saloon. He came out after three hours of gambling and drinking. He staggered his way across the street to the Lazy K Saloon. He didn't stay there long. At about one o'clock he walked down the street to his hotel to turn in for the night. It was an early Sunday morning so the activity in the streets was fairly heavy. I figured that night would be perfect to do the job. My plan was simple. I'd move into position at about 8:30 P.M. to the rear of the horse's stable that was located next to the hotel where the operative lived. I would conceal myself in the shadows of the loft until the operative approached the hotel to retire for the night. I'd do the job before he entered the hotel. I would then make my escape through the alleys back through the town of Deadwood, and then to wherever destiny took me.

I rode into town somewhere between 8:30 and 8:45 P.M. It was a Sunday night and the streets were clear of human traffic. Music from the saloons could be heard. The visibility was excellent because the moon was full. The Winking Lizard Saloon was the only saloon that was open, because business must had been too slow. At 9:00 I saw the operative walk inside the saloon. I cushioned the loft floor so I could lay down on. I had a long time to wait, so I took a nap. I fell into a deep sleep. I dreamed about all the friends that I had made through the years. I thought about my best friends. I dreamed that I was having a conversation with Captain Faulkner. It was a strange dream because nobody responded. In fact, I did all the talking. I dreamed about the good times that John and I used to have during basic training. The nightmare of the dream was amplified immediately by gunfire by McDowell and the operative. As they annihilated everyone that I knew, they laughed uncontrollably.

I woke up in a cold sweat. The dream triggered the beast

within me to come out. To hell with any well thought out plan. I decided to do this the old fashion way. This attitude that the punishment must fit the crime was justified in my mind. I immediately grabbed my double-barreled shotgun and stuffed some shells in my pocket. My patience with the whole mess had reached its climax.

I loaded my shotgun as I approached the pouch of the saloon. I glanced through the double doors of the saloon to see if the operative was there. He was, sitting down gambling with three others. A bar-girl was snuggled up around the operative, sharing the successful monetary gains of his card game. The bartender was positioned behind the bar, shining a glass and observing the card game. The room was dimly lit and cigar smoke dominated the smell. There were no others in the immediate area, except for a loving couple on the steps, intimately lip-locked and about to make their way upstairs to the bedroom. I backed off, locked both triggers of my shotgun, and loosened my holstered 45. I peeped through the window to see if the loving couple had made their way upstairs. Finally, they disappeared. Strangely enough, I hesitated. An internal conflict was brewing. One part of my subconscious was saying, "Don't do it, because killing won't bring back my dead friends." The more dominant part of my subconscious was saying, "Justice must be done." I took a deep breath and weighed the options. I realized that it was too late to turn back. The transformation was complete. I had morphed into an obsessive, insensitive, vengeful killer that lived for revenge. I was no longer responsible for my actions, and I didn't care about the consequences. The only things and people that I cared about were either humiliated or butchered by the McDowells or the Carloses of the world. It was a the sign of the times: men ruled by the gun. Thus, I figured it was time to make my mark in society. I kicked the double doors open and walked into the bar with my shotgun in the ready position. My shotgun was aimed at the four men at the gambling table. I approached them, walking at a slow methodical pace. They quickly stood up. Their eyes were transfixed with horror as I made my way closer to them. One man had his back turned to me, fell back down in his chair, clumsily tipping over the table. The other two men that were seated to the flank of the operative, slowly backed up as they kept their eyes on me. I quickly cut my eyes in the direction of the bartender. He was frozen in position behind the bar, watching my every move. The bar girl was hugged behind the operative. Everyone in the saloon was stunned with fascinated horror. Before anyone could move, I quickly said to the terrified group, "Nobody moves anymore. Mr. Bartender, move back over on this side so I can see you. Anybody that moves is a dead man." I looked at the operative, as he watched me with a disbelieving look. "Was it worth it?" I asked him.

He looked at me with a confused look. "Worth what? What are you talking about?" he asked.

"Was it worth this?" I squeezed both triggers, blasting both the operative and the bar-girl into the walls and onto the floor. Two of the three men went for their weapons, as I dropped my shotgun to pull out my 45s. We all fired at the same time. My 45 bullets struck one man in the head and the other in the chest. Unfortunately, one of their bullets hit me in the side just below my armpit. The others watched in horror. I began to back up to make my exit. I could feel the bullet that was lodged in my side. The warm blood began to drain from my wound. I knew that it was going take every ounce of strength to escape. I looked back at the carnage that I had created. Four individuals lay dead. I looked at the operative once more. His corpse rekindled my vengeful spirit. I fired three more rounds into his corpse to send a clear message to anyone that decided to follow me. Obviously, the message was clear because they stayed paralyzed with horror. I catapulted through the door and quickly withdrew back to my horse. It was difficult for me to mount my horse. The pain in my side was throbbing. I doubled over in agony from the burning sensation left from the bullet. I stuffed my handkerchief in the wounded area, hoping that it would stop the bleeding. I could not use my left shoulder. I believed the bullet must have broken my shoulder blade. I quickly galloped out of town. The pain was so great that I rode most of the way with my eyes closed.

12:30 16TH MARCH

I finally reached the town of Deadwood after about an hour of riding. As I advanced through the streets of Deadwood, I could no longer sit upright on my saddle. My shirt was drenched with blood and I began to grow cold. My conscience faded in and out. A new pain developed when I coughed. I could taste my own blood. Oh...the pain.

12:35 16TH MARCH

Marshall Carr had just finished checking the door of the Kitty Hawk Saloon that was locked for the night. He was making sure because the night before someone had vandalized the saloon, and made off with ten bottles of whiskey. As he looked through the glass window of the saloon, he saw a reflection of me doubled over on my horse. He promptly turned around to see if it was someone that he knew. I galloped past Carr in the direction leading out of town. I was completely delirious from loss of blood. My natural instinct carried me through Deadwood, but nothing would be able to help me much longer if he remained in this current condition. At the time, the Marshall didn't know that it was me that was doubled over the horse, and yet he felt that the clue that he'd been waiting for nine months ago had just proceeded past him.

Marshall Carr followed his instincts. I had no idea that I was being followed. Finally after riding a quarter of a mile I fainted and fell off my horse. I tried to mount his horse but was unsuccessful, and clumsily fell back to the ground. In fact I could no longer move. Marshall Carr emerged upon my weak, blood soaked body. I saw the marshall but was too weak to move. The marshall cautiously looked at me. He pulled out his 38 pistol and aimed it at me. I watched but couldn't respond. The marshall realized that it would be no contest. Marshall Carr kept his gun pointed at me. He kept one eye on me and one eye on my horse. He saw the double barrel shotgun, the 30.06. mounted on the horse. He then made the connection of the unsolved murders that took place at the McDowell's ranch nine months ago. He was confident that I was his man. He was convinced I was the man that blew away five of McDowell's men in his town nine months ago.

He marveled, "One man,… only one man, did all this murdering." Two days later I woke up locked up in Deadwood jail.

The Location: Deadwood Jail Cell

I woke up smelling fresh brewed coffee. The hole in my shoulder had been patched and my arm was in a sling. The marshall brought me a cup of coffee.

"Drink this. It'll make you feel better," the Marshall said. I sat up in my bunk. The marshall handed me the cup in between the bars of the jail cell. The marshall brought over a wooden chair and sat down next to my jail cell. "Answer this one question. Why?"

I paused, smelled the coffee and allowed the aroma to trigger my thoughts. "It's a long story Marshall."

The marshall replied, "I've got nothing but time on my hands." After about three hours and five cups of coffee, I told the marshall why McDowell had been targeted. I also explained to him the circumstances surrounding the sheriff's murder. To confirm my story, I also told him where he could find the mass grave site that McDowell and his men had dug. The marshall decided to keep everything silent. The only one that knew about my incarceration was the doctor that treated me and Marshall Carr. The marshall wanted to keep it quiet because he wanted to have the opportunity to confirm my story.

Later that night, the marshall returned. The doctor stopped him in the middle of the street. His investigation about the truth was undeniable. However, he wasn't sure how he could tie in McDowell's responsibility with these atrocities. The doctor shocked the marshall with new developments that had unfolded during his absence. As a result of my conflict with the operative, McDowell's paranoia level reached a new heights. However, this time McDowell had the legal right to hunt me. Witnesses from the saloon stated that they saw me gun down the innocent white bargirl. This homicidal act enraged the white society. Lynch mobs had been formed. The bounty had been doubled for my capture. To make matters worse, the regional military post had been mobilized. This time McDowell held all the cards. The marshall hurriedly opened the jail-cell. He was sincere in letting me know what he stood for.

"Your story is true, the fact remains that there would be no way that I could tie McDowell in with these atrocities. McDowell is much bigger than I. Hell, he's probably going to be the next governor of the state. I've always known of his illegal activity, but he had too much muscle for me to do anything about it. You guys did me a favor by cleaning out Buford. I am truly indebted for what you guys did. The citizens are truly indebted for getting their town back and under control. Unfortunately, I'm caught in a dilemma. There is no way that I can help you. I know that white girl you killed in the bar was an accident, but you're in the south and there is no court in the US that is gonna vindicate your innocence. I don't have the assets to stop lynching mobs. I don't have the authority to stop army officials. In fact if I'm caught harboring you, I'll probably be hung. The best thing that I could do for you and me is to let you go. I don't know or even care how you plan to escape, but please get the hell out of my town. And, if you come back this way, I'll shoot you myself and collect the reward money."

The marshall handed me my weapons. I hurriedly left Deadwood, never to return again.

CHAPTER 11

HOW FAR IS FAR

ONE YEAR LATER BOSTON MASSACHUSETTS 1880

It took two months to get out of South Carolina. I navigated at night and slept during the day. Time was taking a toll on, not only me, but everything that I owned. I could no longer use my shotguns because the springs in the trigger mechanism broke. I couldn't risk going into any town to get any type of equipment. I was low on money and food. There was a scrimmage line that covered all of the Southeast territory. Therefore, I made my way Northeast. I made Boston my new temporary home. Boston was a large cosmopolitan city. I figured that I could live there and nobody would ever find me. The way of life there was totally different than what I was accustomed to living, and like a chameleon, I changed colors with my environment. I worked in a steel mill for many months. Once again, like the Brunswick Georgia ShipYards, I blended in with the multicultural population. I had begun to make friends and become a part of the community. I was accepted by many and started to establish a worthy relationship with a female companion. Things, places and people that were dear to me usually don't last long.

One evening when I was walking home after a hard day of work, I noticed that a man was questioning my tenants about something. I assumed by the way he was dressed that he was a bounty hunter. His being heavily armed gave his identity away. He stuck out like a sore thumb. He was a bounty hunter, and he had tracked me down. I sneaked my way to the rear of the house in order to get my guns. As I was strapping up my belts, the bounty hunter began to get irate with my friendly tenants. I heard the bounty hunter say, "I want to know where the nigger boy is located." He looked at the old man and said, "You're gonna tell me where I can find the nigger boy, or I'm gonna put a bullet in the bitch's head," he said, referring to the old lady. They were frightened, but they felt compelled not to give away their own people. "You've got till the count of three," the bounty hunter flashed a snobbish grin. I slowly walked out the front door to face this asshole. I gave him a scorching look. The bounty hunter's eyes widened with alarm, and his facial muscles twitched nervously. The sight of this maggot had adrenaline pulsating in my hands. I scraped out the words between clenched teeth, "Oh, I'm sorry. Don't let me interrupt. You were saying something about the count of three. You yellow belly clodhopping redneck, you probably can't count to three, you dumb son of a bitch." The bounty hunter started to dismount his horse. "Get back on that goddam horse, you jackass," I yelled at the top of my voice. He stopped midways through his dismount, and remounted. My eyes were narrowed with contempt, and I said to the bounty hunter, "I figured I'd save you the trouble of dismounting. You'll be dead before you hit the ground." The bounty hunter realized that I was trying to pick a fight. I knew that the bounty hunter would try his luck. There was a long pause. The bounty hunter twitched. Before the bounty hunter could draw his weapons, I unloaded two slugs in the bounty hunter's chest, propelling him off of his horse. He was dead before he hit the ground. Once again I was on the run. I gave the old couple my horse and boarded a cattle car that was heading West. I didn't care about its destination.

CHAPTER 12

DOMICILE

I woke up from a deep sleep. The train slowed down to a grinding halt. I could see the sunshine through the boxcar cracks. After about a week of traveling, I decided to take my chances with this particular territory. I opened the boxcar door. The sunshine broke the darkness. I was temporally blinded. I wiped my eyes to get a better look. What I had seen was simply breathtaking. Land stretched out as far as I could see. It wasn't as green as the hills of Tennessee, but the land itself looked like a distant brownish green carpet and the sun glaze gave it an orange backdrop. I felt a true inner bliss of euphoria that had escaped me years ago. Somehow I knew that that would become my tentative home. I figured the train must have stopped to fuel up with water, but it stopped to unload cattle. I quickly ducked and hid in some bushes near the track. The train moved out shortly afterwards. After the dust cleared, I noticed a town at a distance. I figured that I'd have nothing to lose or gain so I decided to investigate. I had no idea where I was, but I felt comfortable that I was far from my past pandemonium. For now I was contented to stay still until nightfall.

    I woke up and listened to the distant wolves howling. Somehow that howling noise brought on a sort of harmonic distortion that was pleasant to my ears, or maybe I was just tired of listening to the blasting of my shot guns and the distinct popping sounds of my pistols. Looking out over the distant horizons, I could see the faces of the dead. I quickly snapped out of this hypnotic daydreaming state.

Dusk had begun to settle and I started my way towards town.The town's distance was an illusion. I thought the town was only three to four miles away, but I walked for at least four hours before I reached the outskirts of town. I hoped that the illusion wasn't an omen.

I noticed a sign that identified the town. The name of the town was Ballard. I finally made it to my destination, and did not know what the next step was going to be. I felt hollow inside. I felt relieved that I was somewhere, but I was lost in a abyss, caught in a seamless web, spun by the God all mighty himself. I felt free but constrained in the large confines of confusion. The midnight breeze from the desert settled my nerves. The moon was full and the stars were at full sparkle. I didn't have that nasty sticky feeling over my skin caused by the southern swampy humidity. The night life was in a state of calmness when I arrived. The streets must have been dusty during the day, because I was covered with dust. I could taste that crunchy taste of dirt in my mouth. Torches, lanterns illuminated some storefronts, but the alleys were dark and lifeless. I could hear activity coming from the saloons. In one large saloon, I could hear jovial laughter and a piano playing in the background. I wanted to look but I didn't want to attract any unnecessary attention. I started to walk in the opposite direction towards the other saloon. The doors opened suddenly and people began to plow out. The women were dressed in nice silk and satin clothing. The men were dressed in tuxedos. I figured this saloon must be some type of theatre. I ducked into the shadows of the alley between the store and the theatre. Seeing these well-to-do people made me feel uneasy. I wasn't sure if I felt deprived from material things such as nice attire, or just envy. My alter ego began to surface. It was a feeling of hostility, or anger. In any case, I watched the crowd disburse and leave in different directions. I waited until they had all left the area. My curiosity took over. I had to have a look to see what a real drama stage looked like. I was mystified by what was seen. The stage was still bright with lights. The props that surrounded the stage were amazing. I sat in total awe. Suddenly, there was a throbbing sensation on my shoulder, I was being awakened from my daydream. In total panic, I instinctively drew my 45s, turned around, and locked back the triggers, all in one motion. This time I went into total state of amazement at what I saw. There he stood, with a patch over one eye and an arm amputated from the shoulder down. His face showed of the aging process however, he was well dressed and had the look of a politician. It was the man with that touch of class: my old commander. "Lord have mercy on my soul. I thought you were dead sir."

Faulkner replied, "So did Black Jack McDowell. I was wounded and thrown in jail to decompose like some animal. I was supposed to be shot for treason the next day. The president granted me clemency and a new identity. My father used to be a senator in congress and aided me in my quest to become a political figure. I wanted to become a congressman, but my goal fell short. Instead, I'm the mayor of this great metropolis. Want a job? I sure could use your assistance."

My adrenaline rush stopped, and my reflexes caught up with my mind I finally unlocked my triggers and reholstered my 45s. I remained in a state of total awe. The only words that I could muster up were "Why hell yeah." That night I stayed at my old commander's. We talked all night about the status of Ballard. He felt that that the future of Ballard either would boom or bust. In any case, hard times lay ahead, and my special art would be needed. The current sheriff would be retiring within the following months. Also, I would be responsible for recruiting and training a staff of deputies.

It was dawn and the mayor wiped his brow with his one arm and began to talk candidly. "Mack, I want you to change your name, for obvious reasons, of course. Got any suggestions?" We paused momentarily.

I replied, "How about John Smith?"

The Mayor replied "John Doe or John Smith? No that's too plain and common. You need a name that people will remember. You need a name with substance and character. You know, a name that grabs one by the nuts."

I joking said, "How about Harry Hippo?" We laughed but got back on track. I continued, "They'll be shocked anyway because I'm a black man with authority. How about Stanely? Stanley Winston. Stanley the Mack Winston." Mack officially died in Tennessee.

Faulkner retorted, "Stanley, when you take over the sheriff's position, you'll become an extension of me. You will impose my will when needed. I will give you the authority to do what makes things right, whatever, and whenever, and by any means necessary. You will have my full support. I'll have the current sheriff swear you in as his assistant tomorrow. There will be some resistance for this move, but we'll deal with these challenges together. The unique characteristic about Ballard is that it is a large melting pot of people. It's a land of opportunity in a primitive sense. People should be able to live in a free society that offers opportunity and growth. That is my philosophy about life. You and I have seen the worst of worst, and if we allow thugs and such as the Carlos and McDowells to go unchallenged, we'll always live in a world of shit. You're blessed with the tools necessary to meet Ballard's future challenges. We are the last of the elite buffalos. You can make a difference, Stanley. Stanley, you're the man. I want you to consider Ballard your home. There's no reason for you to drift. Life is too short. There's a difference between life and existence."

I immediately thought about what my mother said to me when I worked in the tobacco fields. I thought to myself "It's my turn. It's my turn to make things right."